Hot tears spilled down her face as she thought of Sam, how he would take all of this on himself. But it was her fault. She shouldn't have gone with the man.

She wouldn't.

She stopped, turned toward her assailant, the barrel of the gun near her eye.

He didn't want to kill her here. Knew he'd be caught.

"Move!" he growled, and a door above them slammed open.

"Kathryn!"

Sam. Coming down the stairs!

The man yanked her back, hand fisting painfully in her hair, gun pressed to the side of her head.

Footsteps echoed, fast along the metal steps. Sam turned the corner, weapon drawn.

He met Kat's eyes, and she wondered if this would be their last moment together.

SARA K. PARKER

was raised in central Maryland and spent many childhood hours with her nose in a book or a pen in hand. The youngest of five children, she longed to grow up, and began pursuing a writing career at the age of fifteen. That year, her first poem was published in a Christian magazine, and Sara has continued to weave her faith into most of her writing. Sara holds an undergraduate degree in journalism and a master's degree in writing. She and her husband stay busy with four children, three dogs and a cat in a suburb near Houston, Texas. When she's not writing or wrangling children or animals, Sara spends her time teaching piano, reading, reorganizing or experimenting in the kitchen.

UNDERCURRENT
SARA K. PARKER

HARLEQUIN® LOVE INSPIRED® SUSPENSE

Recycling programs
for this product may
not exist in your area.

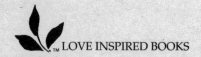 LOVE INSPIRED BOOKS

ISBN-13: 978-0-373-44646-9

Undercurrent

www.Harlequin.com

Printed in U.S.A.

I will lead the blind by ways they have not known,
along unfamiliar paths I will guide them;
I will turn the darkness into light before them
and make the rough places smooth.
—*Isaiah* 42:16

To my mom and dad, Shirley and Edward Porter.
I still remember opening that electric keyboard
one glorious Christmas morning—thank you
for always encouraging me to pursue my dreams.

To my husband, Nate, who never doubted, tirelessly
helping with kids and housework so I could write.
I love you, and I couldn't have done this without you.

To my sister, Shirlee McCoy, a critique partner
who tells it like it is until we're laughing so hard
we're crying. You said I'd get here,
and you believed it. Thank you.

And to God, who orchestrated it all.

ONE

Someone had been in her stateroom.

Blue sapphire organza spilled out of the opened garment bag in Kathryn Brooks's closet. She hadn't touched it since the day they'd set sail, when she'd carefully hung the gown alongside her other performance attire. Kat was meticulous about her work clothes, had to be, considering their hefty price tag. She never would have left one of her bags open. Especially not the one holding her Jovani gown, the one her dad had bought for her.

So, who had opened it?

The question gripped her and wouldn't let go.

She checked the zipper along the edge of the white casing, found it intact. She glanced around the room.

Everything else looked just the way she'd left it when she'd gone to the gym. The bed had been made, though, and a towel folded into the shape of a monkey hung from the ceiling. Johann's doing.

She still felt funny about the special treatment, but her agent had insisted on requesting a room with a balcony, a steward and all the perks that vacationing travelers enjoyed.

It was how a world-renowned concert pianist traveled, Becky Landry had told her. "In style."

Kat unhooked the gown from its hanger and carried it to

the bed, laid it out atop the white down comforter. Traced the seams, checked the hem. No harm done.

Perhaps her cabin steward had just been curious. If it happened again, she'd have a word with him. She chided herself for her paranoia.

She needed to get a handle on that. Ever since the fire, she'd been battling anxiety.

Rooming with her best friend had been the perfect antidote. During the day, Morgan was the best kind of company—funny and adventurous, always dragging Kat out of their room to explore new ports and socialize with passengers. And during the quiet hours of the night, Kat was never alone. But Morgan had disembarked for a family emergency four days ago, leaving Kat right back in the very place she'd sought to escape—alone with her thoughts.

The room was stuffy. She left the gown and opened the glass balcony door, stepped out to the railing. Hot wind assaulted her, mid-July sun beating down without mercy. She welcomed the heat, its warmth on her face, the pungent saltiness of the sea—all reminders that she was alive. Just three months ago, she'd wondered if she'd ever feel the sun again, see the crisp blue sky, inhale the scents of summer.

Absently, she traced a hand down her left side, the ridges of the bandage smoothing down under her fingertips. The fire had licked a three-inch-wide path from midthigh to the bottom of her rib cage. In time, the burn would fade, but the scar would remain forever. None of it mattered, though, compared to what she had lost.

Kat blinked hard and shut out the regrets.

She wouldn't look back. Not with all the beauty stretched out before her. The *Jade Princess* lulled gently, no land in sight. Four days since leaving port in Salvador de Bahia, Brazil, the ship floated leisurely toward its next destination, the Canary Islands. Kat breathed in the ocean breeze, trying to drum up the thrill of the adventure ahead. But all she felt was the ache of all that had been.

Her dad would have loved cruising. She could picture him walking the promenade and talking up his only child's accomplishments to anyone who would listen. It hurt to know he'd spent his entire life working, until one day he couldn't.

A massive stroke in November had pushed him out of the state's attorney's office and into disability retirement. Kat had canceled her tour and moved back into the house she'd grown up in. Cared for her dad and willed him to get better while she took a faculty piano instructor position at the University of Miami.

Her father had started to improve, gaining back motion on the right side of his body, carrying on brief conversations. They'd begun to connect in a way Kat had craved since her mother had died. They'd eaten dinner together most nights, classical music in the background, reminiscing and dreaming. He wanted to travel, he told her, once he was back on his feet. She said she'd go with him as soon as his doctor okayed the trip.

But in January, he had another stroke. Kat was at work when it happened. Found him on the floor by his bed when she came home. Too late.

Setting her gaze on the horizon, still and unreachable, Kat clenched the railing, determined. Before her mother passed away fourteen years ago, Kat had made a promise that she would keep putting one foot in front of the other, even when it hurt.

Especially when it hurt.

She'd done just that, and now here she was, on her third job of a six-cruise contract as a concert pianist. She had to hand it to Morgan. The timing had been ripe for this kind of adventure.

The home she'd grown up in had burned to the ground in March, nearly taking her with it. When she was released from the burn center, bandages still covering ugly scars, footsteps slow with pain and heavy from loss, Kat knew it was up to her to make a new beginning.

The rebuild of Kat's childhood home would be complete by the time her contract ended, and she'd be able to stop living out of suitcases. In the meantime, she'd have a chance to gain some perspective and evaluate what she would do with her career.

Halfway through her contract, Kat didn't feel refreshed and she hadn't gained a new perspective or figured out her next course, but at least she was keeping her promise to keep moving forward.

Her watch beeped.

Time to get to work.

She left the balcony door open as she reentered the cabin, hoping to gather the scent of the sea.

Her gaze flitted over Morgan's bed, concern tugging at the pit of her stomach. Kat picked up her phone and checked it. No updates yet. She hoped everything was okay. Morgan's brother, Jake, was in the hospital again, and this time it was serious. For Jake, a twenty-nine-year-old cystic fibrosis patient, any hospital visit could mean the end. Kat sent up a silent prayer for Morgan's brother and then picked her dress up from the bed.

A flutter of familiar anticipation coursed through her. She always felt it right before a performance. Her cruise contract promised an adventure of a lifetime, and Kat was determined to embrace it.

Samuel West took a sip of black coffee and wondered, not for the first time, how his siblings had managed to pin him down for this one. Whatever their methods, they had succeeded, and now he sat watching rippling dark water against clear blue skies while keeping the corner of his eye trained on the woman who brought trouble wherever she set foot.

Grandma.

Ever since Grandpa Frank had died last year, Grandma had been on what could only be described as a travel binge. After her first trip left her stranded in Italy with no passport and her second trip ended before it had even begun, with a nasty fall on the airport escalator that fractured her wrist, Sam and his five siblings had gathered with Mom to devise a plan.

Grandma relished her independence, and her mind was still as sharp as ever, but she couldn't be trusted to embark on adventures alone. Together the family made a pact to take turns joining Grandma Alice on her vacations.

Sam could think of a host of other things he'd rather do than hang out on a cruise ship. Too confined and predictable. But it was his turn, Grandma had told him with her no-nonsense voice, and she knew he had the vacation time available. Knew he hadn't taken a day off in two years.

A flash of blue drew his gaze away from his grandmother and up to the wide spiral staircase at the center of the atrium. A woman stood still and graceful on the steps, near-black hair cascading down past her shoulders. Like a figure in a painting, she posed with serenity, one hand resting on the polished brass railing, the other relaxed at her side, gown shimmering under the chandeliers that lit the lobby.

"It's six o'clock, and we on the *Jade Princess* trust that you're enjoying your voyage across the Atlantic Ocean to the Canary Islands and then on to Malaga, Spain." The loud voice on the sound system filtered throughout the atrium as patrons wandered through the area and into the coffee shop and art gallery across the way. "In case you missed last night's classical performance by concert pianist Kathryn Brooks, she will perform again in just a moment in the atrium. Ms. Brooks is a Florida native who made her debut at Carnegie Hall at the age of fifteen and has traveled the world delighting audiences ever since. She's performed at Steinway Hall and the Sydney Opera House, and now we have the privilege of listening to her performances along our journey. Make sure to pass through the atrium on deck eight to hear her breathtaking music."

Sam's attention fastened on the woman in blue as she took the last few steps to the lobby and made her way to the shiny black grand piano set to the left of a wide center stage. Her black heels tapped against the white marble floor, and the din in the room hushed.

Passersby seemed drawn to the woman as she took her seat on a leather-cushioned bench, the flowing fabric of her gown caressing the floor at her feet. She turned slightly toward the audience, speaking into the microphone at her side.

"Good evening," she said. "I hope you're all enjoying your sea voyage as much as I am." Her voice carried clearly through the lobby, mellow and sweet. A few people clapped in agreement and she smiled.

She pushed a lock of hair behind her ear. A narrow streak of white appeared and disappeared so quickly Sam wasn't sure he'd actually seen it.

"I'm often asked if music runs in the family. If my parents were here tonight, they'd laugh at the question. In church, my mother worked hard to master lip-synching to hymns, while the rest of the congregation wished my father would, too."

Sam found himself smiling along with the rest of her captive audience. *Magnetic* was how he would describe her. And gorgeous.

"But my parents' failure to carry a tune didn't stand in their way of bringing music into our home," she continued. "I recall many dinners with the CD player as background music. One night we might listen to Elvis, the next the latest Christian artist and another night an orchestral production. We would scour the thrift shops and clearance boxes at a little music store in town, always searching for something we hadn't heard before." She played a few sweet, slow notes and soft laughter rippled through the audience as they recognized "Twinkle, Twinkle, Little Star."

"I suppose that's where my love of music began, and I credit my mother for inspiring me. While I can lose myself in a Chopin nocturne or a Brahms lullaby, I've always craved the challenge of creating, taking something beautiful and…changing it up a little."

She turned away from the microphone, made a swift key change and began an arrangement of "Twinkle, Twinkle, Little Star" unlike any Sam had ever heard before. Her hands flew over the keys, turning the lullaby into a jazzy rendition that brought cheers from her growing audience. It was a short piece, and it came to an abrupt stop, met with enthusiastic applause. The woman turned back to the microphone.

"Tonight I'll be performing some pieces you'll probably all be familiar with. I hope you'll enjoy my interpretation. If not, I understand that there's plenty to do on ship. Which is a good thing, considering we have three more days before we hit our next destination."

Even the young children in the room sat quietly watching, captivated by her

"In honor of our grand adventure, I wonder if you'll recognize this first tune."

Sam did right away—"What a Wonderful World"—and he observed the faces of bystanders as they murmured to each other.

The pianist's graceful movements drew Sam in, her eyes closing briefly at the most tender sounds in the piece. Simple notes strung together into tangible emotion beneath the movement of her hands. Her energy and passion for her music flowed through the room, which had suddenly grown more crowded.

The song was one of Grandma's favorites, and Sam glanced to his right, expecting to spot her big red hat swaying to the rhythm.

She wasn't there.

He bit back a sigh and stood up, gaze roaming the room. Even in a hall thick with passengers, locating his grandmother should be a cinch with that enormous hat of hers. He moved from his seat, and a young couple scooped up his small round table as he entered the throng of people.

There. The red hat. He caught a glimpse as his grandmother entered the art gallery.

He took a step toward her, but something in his periphery caught his attention. Not the crowds shuffling through, not the toddler getting restless in his stroller, but a sudden shift in the air. Something wasn't right.

His eyes caught on a figure moving swiftly out of the atrium and into the coffee shop. Dark jeans, a black ball cap and a black jacket. He stood out in the atmosphere of leisure, where the only others rushing about were uniformed crew.

The man was probably just in a rush to meet up with someone. Still, a chill of foreboding kicked Sam's pulse up a notch, and his gaze sharpened as it traveled over the sea of crew and passengers. He'd had this feeling many times before. Not a premonition. Just gut instinct. Grandma would say it was a nudge from God, and Sam wouldn't argue with that. But this was more like being clubbed in the head. A very strong warning.

A few feet away, the pianist's hands pulsed over the

keys with precision and speed, the giant chandelier glimmering above the piano.

Adrenaline coursed through Sam, years of training kicking in as he mentally logged the technical details of his surroundings. The room easily held five hundred people with several dozen onlookers from above. Six points of entry, ten including the elevators.

He looked up, slowly scanned the faces of the people looking over the railings upstairs. The volume was intense, voices chattering, piano clamoring, china clinking from a nearby restaurant.

Pop!

That one sound carried over all the others. Sparks flew from the chandelier above the piano and smoke poured from the ceiling.

The music stopped.

Hundreds of people pushing, running. Screaming.

He saw her, the woman in the sapphire gown, right as her eyes drew upward, horror written on her face. Instinct and training carried him to the stage as the pianist fumbled to escape, tripped up by her gown. A loud crack. A burst of flame. The chandelier broke away from its mount two stories above the center stage just as Sam's feet hit the marble.

Kat's heel caught the hem of her gown. She fell to her knees, scrambling to get away. From the rocking chandelier, the raining sparks, the thick smoke.

Strong arms wrapped around her, everything a blur as she rolled from the stage. A deafening crash, and screams and chaos erupted all around. She was pinned, facedown, by a complete stranger, smoke stinging her nose and filling her lungs.

She needed to get out. *Now.* She jerked upward, the back of her head making contact with a hard jaw. Pain seared through her, and the man stood, dragging Kat to her feet.

His hand held firmly onto her arm, urgency etched in the taut lines of his face. "Are you hurt?"

"No," she managed, willing her body to steady itself. A firm arm wrapped around her back.

"Come on!" The man tugged her away from the crowd of fleeing people and back toward the piano, the smoke, the shards of chandelier.

Fear paralyzed her, memories of another fire reeling her back, and Kat tried to yank away from his grip, but he wouldn't let go. Smoke billowed through the cavernous room; flames licked the ceiling. And she was back in her bedroom months ago, trapped by fire scorching the walls, clawing for her, bright, hot, ravenous.

"The other way is too crowded!" the stranger shouted over the chaos in the atrium, and Kat forced herself to focus on him. "This is the safer route."

He was right. Most people had run from the crash toward the stairwell and elevators. Hundreds clogged the exits behind them, shoving and pushing and panicking. They could more easily exit through the art gallery or one of the restaurants on the opposite side.

The stranger guided her carefully and quickly along the edge of the atrium, just yards away from the chandelier, broken into millions of shards of crystal and metal. It had obliterated the Steinway grand. The bench Kat had been sitting on moments before had simply disappeared into the rubble.

An alarm sounded. Loud, repetitive, painful. An announcement, urgent, echoed throughout the ship. She couldn't hear the words over the alarm and the panicked voices ringing around her.

Harsh smoke enveloped them, mingling with a sharp

chemical scent and the foggy mist from the sprinkler system. Kat coughed against the acrid smoke, eyes burning.

"Use this, and stay low." The man at her side thrust a cloth napkin into her hands and pulled her into a crouch as they maneuvered toward an exit.

Kat held the napkin to her face and followed, pushing back images of that fiery night in March, flames clinging to her pajama pants, the walls of her parents' house buckling around her.

She'd lost her heels, and her bare feet slid along the now-slick floor. Their path brought them past toppled chairs and purses left behind, coffee spilled and cameras abandoned on tables.

"Almost there," the man said, his tone calm and even.

If he was scared, he wasn't showing it. As a matter of fact, she had the sense that he knew what he was doing. That he'd done it before or had trained for it. He made no missteps, didn't hesitate, just led her efficiently out of the area and into the art gallery. The smoke wasn't as thick there, the air clearer.

Kat chanced a look back. Security officers descended on the scene as fire crew swarmed in from all directions, aiming a hose and extinguishers at what remained of the flames. The fire was contained.

They were safe.

Kat had escaped death. A second time. She should feel relieved, but a shudder coursed through her, dread in its wake.

TWO

"Grandma!"

Kat jumped at the barked shout and felt the grip on her side loosen. But the man didn't release her.

"Over here!" he called.

She followed his gaze. A trim older woman wearing a very large red hat hurried toward them. She looked to be in her early seventies, and her eyes were lit with interest rather than fear.

"Sam, I'm so glad you're all right." Her gaze cut to Kat, and she smiled. "You're Kathryn Brooks. I heard you playing earlier—just beautiful music!" She glanced past Kat's shoulder. "Looks like the piano didn't survive. What happened?"

Good question. Kat had no idea.

"We need to keep moving," Sam said, taking his grandmother's arm. He started walking, his hand still gripping Kat's wrist. She pulled away.

"I'm okay now." She could make it back to her room without help.

Gray eyes turned to her, assessing.

"Your color may be coming back, but I'd like to stay close until you're settled in your room."

His gaze lingered a moment, and Kat's cheeks heated in response as she made a mental note of the details she would relay to Morgan once this nightmare was over. Eyes the color of steel. A couple days' worth of growth on a strong jaw. And biceps that stretched the edging on the sleeves of his black polo.

"Really, I'll be okay getting to my room," she murmured, tempted to accept his offer but not wanting to impose on Sam and his grandmother. In truth, she'd rather not be alone after what had just happened.

"Humor me," Sam said, and Kat wondered if he could read the fear in her eyes. "I'd like to make sure you get back to your cabin in one piece." He didn't leave room for argument, turning abruptly and leading his grandmother through the narrow gallery.

Kat followed. They were heading for the stairwell she needed anyway.

"How in the world did that chandelier fall?" Sam's grandmother asked.

"It didn't fall," Sam said. "It exploded."

Kat shivered. "And landed right where I was sitting. Your grandson saved my life," she added.

She didn't think Sam had heard her. His focus was fixed on the winding staircase ahead, where passengers had begun to clog the stairwells. Energy nearly vibrated from the man as he patiently matched pace with his grandmother, cupping her elbow as they ascended the steps. It was a rare man who cared so deeply for his grandmother.

Movement on the stairs was slow going, but at least most people seemed calm. More calm than Kat felt, anyway.

Sam was right. It had been an explosion, but surely it was accidental. An electrical problem, perhaps? She glanced at Sam, noticed the way he continually scanned the crowd. As if he sensed more danger was coming. The thought urged her to go faster, and she pressed in closely behind Sam and his grandmother.

"I'm not surprised he saved you," his grandmother said. "That's what my Sammy does."

"Saves lives?" Kat stole a glance at him.

"Yes," his grandmother said cheerfully. "He's a bona fide hero."

"Grandma." The word was a warning, but Sam's grandmother didn't seem at all concerned about heeding it.

"It's what God put him here to do. And I think He's proving that today."

"Grandma, really. *Enough*," Sam ground out, shooting his grandmother a look of half exasperation and half amused tolerance.

"Fine. If I must, I'll stop telling her about you. For now," she said with an innocent smile. "I'm Alice West, by the way."

"It's good to meet you, Alice," Kat responded. "Though circumstances could be better."

"They could also be worse," Alice said.

True. Kat could be dead. The passengers in the atrium this evening could have been injured. The fire could have spread quickly through the ship. They could all be fighting over lifeboats at this very moment.

So many things could have been worse, and Kat tried to hold on to that. Morgan would call her a pessimist, but Kat was simply realistic. And there was no escaping the fact that she'd narrowly escaped death twice now, and she could happily do without another near-death experience.

She shuddered, wishing they could move a little faster. She couldn't wait to reach the safety of her room. Kat glanced at Sam. He seemed on high alert, and she was curious about what his grandmother had divulged. She'd stopped believing in heroes a long time ago, but he seemed like the kind of guy who just might renew her faith.

"What floor are you on, Kat?" he asked without looking her way.

"Twelve."

"Oh my," Alice said with a glint in her eyes. "What a lovely coincidence. We are, too."

"Grandma," Sam cut in, his gaze still tracking the movement of the people in front of him. "How about you—"

"Attention all crew and passengers!"

The announcement sounded clearly through the speakers overhead, and voices in the stairwell hushed as passengers strained to listen. "This is Captain Philip Orland. As many of you know, there has been a fire in the atrium. We have the situation under control but ask that you proceed to your staterooms immediately until further notice, to clear the hallways and public areas for our crew to work. I want to assure you that we have highly trained fire and security crews here on the *Jade Princess*. The fire is out, and the damage was limited to the atrium. You can feel safe tonight."

"How reassuring," Alice said softly, and Kat smiled at the hint of sarcasm. Alice's tone reminded her of Morgan's dry sense of humor. Her best friend and Sam's grandmother would have probably really hit it off.

"Room number?" Sam asked as they exited the stairwell.

"Twelve fifty-three," Kat answered.

Alice looked thoughtfully at Kat. "I always thought the performers on cruise ships roomed with the crew."

"Usually they do," Kat said. "The room was negotiated into my contract."

"You must be something special in the music world." Alice grinned.

"I don't know about that, but I have a great agent who likes to see just how much she can squeeze out of each of my contracts."

"A balcony is worth that kind of effort, I'd say," Sam's

grandmother said. "My Sammy played the piano for a few years." Her eyes twinkled, and Kat had the distinct impression that Alice was on a mission. A mission to play matchmaker. And Kat didn't want any part of it, especially not in the midst of what was happening on the ship.

She'd venture to guess Sam didn't, either. He seemed determined to ignore his grandmother's comment.

"Did he?"

"Oh, yes, but it was a battle to get him to practice. Whenever I was in charge of the kids, I'd have to stand over Sam or he would slip out of the house before I could catch him. And now look at us—he's the one standing over me! The family sent him to babysit me, you know."

Kat bit her lip to keep from laughing at the woman's indignant expression.

"Grandma," Sam said and sighed. "I think you should—"

"Kat!" someone shouted, and she knew without looking who it was.

Max.

Just about the last person in the world she wanted to see. She reigned in her irritation. A journalist for a regional magazine, Max had knocked on her cabin door their second day of cruising. He'd claimed his editor had assigned him a travel piece, but Kat didn't buy it. He wrote for the entertainment department, not travel, and had never written anything else in the fourteen months they'd dated. The fact that his new assignment put him on ship with Kat seemed a little too coincidental.

"Kat!" he called again.

Much as she wanted to ignore him, she felt compelled to wait as he jogged toward her. He sidled up next to her, obvious concern in his blue eyes. Eyes that had once drawn her to him. They *did* have a way of appearing genuine. Even now, she found herself believing he was concerned for her, that he truly did care about her.

He'd proven the opposite, though, back in April when Kat had been in the hospital.

"What happened? Are you okay?" His gaze slid to Sam, who was watching the exchange intently, his gray eyes devoid of emotion. Alice watched, too, her red hat askew, her eyes flashing with interest.

"I'm fine." Her answer was clipped, and she saw a look of hurt pass through Max's eyes. She had never been good at rudeness, and she caved to the puppy-dog expression. "The chandelier above the piano fell in the atrium during my performance. It was a close call."

"I should have been there," he said, and Kat held back a sigh.

She, for one, was glad he hadn't been. He'd sat in the front row of her other three performances on board. She found his presence odd and irritating, being that he'd never shown a huge interest in her career when they were dating. He was tone-deaf, his singing at church rivaling the mournful cry of a hungry calf, and he'd always preferred a loud ball game to a quiet concert. That should have been a red flag, but she'd somehow allowed herself to ignore it.

"Why?" she asked as Sam stopped in front of the door to her room.

"I could have made sure you were okay." He glanced at Sam and frowned.

Kat wished she'd known Max had planned to purchase a ticket on the cruise. She would have made sure her room wasn't on the same deck as his. Ever since the breakup, he'd been campaigning to win her back. But following her aboard the cruise had taken his efforts to a whole new level of obnoxious.

"She was okay, and she still is," Sam cut in. "You should probably do what the captain said and return to your stateroom."

"I'll just make sure she gets settled in her room. Thanks

for walking her here." Max tried to dismiss Sam, but Sam wasn't taking the hint. He leaned against the wall, arms crossed over his chest, dark eyes steady on Kat.

"You want to go ahead and open the door?" he asked, and her cheeks heated.

"Right." She reached for her purse, then realized she didn't have it. "I don't have my keycard. I left it with the concierge before the performance."

"Come on down to my room, Kat," Max suggested, and she almost laughed at his earnestness. As if he was her knight in shining armor instead of a cheating sleaze.

"No." She didn't add *thank you*, though the polite woman her parents had raised her to be demanded it. Morgan would have been proud.

Sam glanced at Max and back to Kat. "Are you traveling with someone who has another keycard?"

Kat shook her head. "No, but please don't worry about me. I don't mind waiting out the time upstairs."

"Nonsense," Alice said. "Come to my room. It's no time to be alone."

"Really, I can—"

"You'd be doing me a favor," Alice insisted. "All this drama has really shaken me." She pressed her hand to her chest and heaved a deep sigh.

"Grandma," Sam warned. "Don't."

"Don't what?" she responded, straightening her hat and brushing her hand down her bright red shorts.

"Act like you're on death's door to get Kathryn to go with you."

"Who says I'm acting?" Alice said. "We're *all* on death's door. Now, come on. To my room. I need to journal everything before I forget it." She grabbed Kat's hand, and Kat didn't have the heart to pull away.

Besides, it didn't seem like the time to argue. Not when the captain had asked everyone to return to their staterooms and not when Kat's legs still felt shaky with the remnants of her fear. And certainly not when Max was watching with the hangdog expression he'd been wearing every time she'd seen him since the cruise had begun.

He caught up with her again, his dark hair ruffled, fists clenched at his sides. It wasn't a good look for him. He'd always been a laid-back kind of guy with a whatever-makes-you-happy attitude. It was one of the things she'd liked about him. But it had been their downfall in the end. He'd done what made him happy, and she couldn't forget it.

"You can go back to your own room, Max." She said the words quietly, trying not to make a scene.

He didn't take the hint. "I'm worried about you, Kat. Let me just walk you to this kind lady's room and—"

"I'm *fine*, Max."

"I think what she means to say is that you're not invited." Sam speared Max with a warning look that stopped her ex in his tracks.

Max glared. She thought he might argue, but true to form, he turned from conflict. "If you change your mind, you know where to find me." He turned on his heel and stalked away.

Sam didn't know who Max was, but he didn't like the guy. As a matter of fact, right at the moment, there were a lot of things he didn't like. He didn't like that Kathryn had almost been killed by a falling chandelier in the atrium. He didn't like that his grandmother was on a cruise ship in the middle of the Atlantic Ocean where there had just been a significant fire. And he didn't like the feeling of unease that had latched on to him right before the explosion and hadn't let up since.

An image flashed through his memory. The man he'd seen hurrying out of the atrium and into the coffee shop.

He'd let Security know about that. Maybe they could pull up footage and get an ID on the guy. Just to be safe.

He led the women to room 1237 and waited impatiently for his grandmother to open the door. He wanted to go back down to the atrium, talk to Security, see if they had any ideas about what had caused the explosion.

Finally, his grandmother managed to dig out her key-card from the oversize bag she was carrying and opened the door.

Kat hesitated at the doorway, and he nudged her forward. He didn't want her wandering around the cruise ship any more than he wanted Grandma doing it. The safest place for both of them was exactly where they were.

THREE

"Well." Alice crossed the room and dropped onto the bed. "I was looking for excitement when I signed up for this cruise, but a falling chandelier and a fire were not what I'd anticipated." She took off her hat and tossed it on the nightstand beside her.

"I'd offer to call for some tea, but my hands are still shaking something fierce," Grandma said.

"It would probably be a while before someone could bring it to us, anyway," Kat said. "Would you like me to make you some?"

"No, no. Tea brewed in a coffee pot always tastes like coffee. But how sweet to offer. You just sit down for a bit. You've been through a trauma, Kathryn."

"Thanks, and you can just call me Kat." She perched on the edge of a brown leather chair, bare feet peeking out from under her gown. Sam caught a glimpse of sparkly silver toenails before she rearranged the hem of her gown to cover her feet. She clasped her hands together in her lap, absently twisting a plain gold band on her right ring finger.

"I wonder how something like this could happen," his grandmother said. She ran a hand along her straight white hair, smoothing it down. She'd given up coloring it long ago and now just bleached it white every now and again.

It was better than gray, she said, and more believable than blond.

"Trouble does seem to follow you, Grandma," Sam said wryly. It'd been a running joke long before he'd joined the family as a troubled foster kid looking for roots. He closed the door with a quiet snap, his gaze settling on Kat.

"Which is why you came to babysit me, right? Imagine that." Alice huffed, her hair nearly vibrating with the force of her indignation. "A seventy-two-year-old being treated like a toddler. It's ridiculous, don't you think, Kat?"

"Well, I…" She met Sam's eyes.

He could tell she wasn't quite sure how to respond to his grandmother.

"Should I remind you that you're the one who insisted I come with you?" he pointed out.

His grandmother huffed again. "That was only because I knew you had more time available than the rest of them." She looked at Kat. "Until this cruise, he hadn't taken a day off in two years!"

He caught the speculation in Kat's gaze. Grandma had a way of turning the conversation back to him, but he had another agenda, and before Kat could comment, he got to it.

"You and Max don't seem friendly. How do you know each other?"

"We dated for a while." She rubbed at a smudge of soot that stained the blue fabric of her dress. He could have told her it would never come out. The fancy dress was tomorrow's trash, which was too bad. But at least Kat was okay.

"And you both just happen to be on the same cruise together, or did you come together and then separate?"

"He's a journalist. He's writing a travel piece for his magazine."

Convenient. The smarmy ex-boyfriend had followed her on board. Why? To get even with her for something?

Rig the chandelier to fall when Kat was performing? Even Sam knew his imagination was stretching there. Any number of things could have caused the explosion, and Max didn't strike him as someone who could successfully plan and implement such an elaborate scheme. The guy probably came on board to try to win Kathryn back. Even so, Sam never operated on assumptions.

"What's his last name? And what magazine does he work for?" At least he could look into the guy, corroborate the reasons for his trip.

"Pratt. Maxwell Pratt. He works for *Miami Motions*." Kat pushed a strand of damp hair away from her shoulder. Whatever makeup she'd been wearing had faded, leaving only traces of mascara smeared under her eyes. The sprinklers had drenched her hair and soaked her gown. She shivered, and Sam snagged a blanket from the end of the bed, tucking it around her shoulders.

"Thanks," she murmured, pulling it closed around her wet dress.

"Looks like your ex-boyfriend is still pining for you," Grandma said, eyes glinting with interest. It would be better if Sam could interview Kat alone, but there was nowhere else to go, and he didn't plan to wait.

"He's been hoping we'll get back together. But it's over," Kat said. He saw the finality in her expression and didn't doubt her words.

"How long did you two date?" Sam asked.

"A little more than a year." She didn't want to talk about Max. He knew it, from her rigid posture, her brief answers. But Sam needed information, and he would get it.

"When did you break up?"

She looked at him then, brow furrowed. "I don't want to be rude, but I'd rather not discuss Max."

"I get that, and I don't mean to pry. I'm just trying to piece together the facts."

Kat's gaze narrowed and she pulled the blanket tighter around her slender frame. "And my relationship with Max matters because…?"

She clearly wasn't following his line of thought, and why would she? Any number of things could have caused the explosion. But Sam's instinct told him whatever the cause, it wasn't accidental.

"It may not matter at all," he said. "But sometimes the smallest details help."

"In this case, I don't see how," Kat insisted. She looked young and vulnerable, and Sam wondered why she was even here. Why would a world-class pianist take a gig on a cruise ship? It certainly couldn't be for the money. Exposure? She didn't seem as if she was desperate for it.

"Don't mind him, Kathryn," Grandma chimed in sweetly from her reclined position on the bed. "This is just who Sam is. That's the problem with his being a Secret Service agent. He always thinks he's on duty." His grandmother looked as if she were watching a movie play out. He was tempted to offer to get her a bag of popcorn and a soda for all her interest in their conversation.

"Secret Service?" Kat met Sam's eyes.

He shrugged as if it weren't a big deal. Maybe to him it wasn't, but it would be more valuable information to supply to Morgan later. Kat smiled as she imagined telling her friend all the details of the day. Knowing Morgan, she'd be disappointed she missed out on all the action. Kat, on the other hand, just wanted to rewind to those moments on the balcony before her performance. When she'd felt tranquil and safe. She didn't enjoy chaos or drama.

"So you live in DC, then?" she asked, latching on to the chance to change the subject.

"No. I'm at the Miami field office," he said, but moved

right on with his objective. "You don't have any enemies, do you?" Sam asked.

The question caught her off guard, and she looked at him seriously, trying to read his expression.

"That's an odd question."

"Not when you were nearly crushed by a chandelier," Sam said.

Connecting the chandelier's fall to foul play was a leap, in Kat's opinion. She opened her mouth to say as much, but Sam suddenly pulled the other chair over and sat across from her. She almost laughed. His grandmother was right. It was as if he was in his own interrogation room with her. Samuel West *did* have the appearance of a Secret Service agent. Not that she'd ever met one. But he fit the image she'd stored in her imagination. Tall, muscled, dark hair, sharp eyes.

Only, he wore blue jeans and a black polo instead of a suit and tie. And they were in the middle of the ocean on a cruise, not back on land in a federal building.

"Enemies?" he prodded.

"None that I know of," Kat said.

"So, you weren't running from something when you took this job?"

"No!" The word came out a little too forcefully, and Kat knew it. She *had* been running from something, she supposed. From loss. Her father, the house, her relationship with Max. All of it, gone.

"Then why did you take it?"

She wanted to tell him it was none of his business, that she'd had enough of the interrogation, and she wanted to call down for her key. But Sam had saved her life, and she owed him more than an ungrateful response.

"It was time for a change. I wanted to try something new. My best friend has been working on cruises for years. She suggested it." There. Simple, but true.

He searched her face, as if he could read her thoughts. She hoped he couldn't, because her attention had been drawn just then to the way his polo stretched across a muscled chest.

"You needed a change from touring the world doing concerts…so you decided to work on a cruise ship. Touring the world, doing concerts."

He saw right through her, she knew. But she didn't want to discuss Dad. The fire. All the other reasons she'd taken the job. She looked into his piercing eyes and knew her efforts were futile.

"I canceled my tour back in November when my dad had a stroke. I moved in with him for a few months and started teaching piano at the University of Miami. My dad passed away in January. I needed a little time away."

She didn't mention the fire. She didn't want sympathy points from anyone. The fact that her house was being rebuilt while she was away was only a small reason she'd left Miami. Max was another. Only he'd still found a way to stay close. She simply wouldn't share everything about her life with a stranger.

Even if that stranger had saved her life.

"I'm sorry about your father," Alice said. "It's hard to lose someone you love."

"Thank you." She stood, unwrapped the blanket from her shoulders and laid it over the back of the chair. "I'd better call for my key. I'd like to get back to my room and out of this dress."

She moved toward the phone, but Sam snagged her hand. She looked back at him, and her breath caught. The tenderness in his gaze tugged at her heart, a deep longing rising from where she'd shoved it away. Longing for constancy, companionship, family.

"I was hoping you'd stay with my grandmother while I talk to ship security down below."

She tugged her hand out of his grasp and set to tying her wet hair back into a low bun. The cool dampness did its job and she pushed her feelings away.

"I do *not* need a babysitter." Alice muttered the words under her breath. Crossed her arms defiantly.

"Noted, Grandma."

Kat looked from Alice to Sam. It was none of her business, but she found herself increasingly curious about this man who had taken leave from work to care for his grandmother on vacation and then taken on Kat's protection as his responsibility. Her cynical side reminded her that people who seemed too good to be true usually were. But the woman in her—the part of her heart that longed for companionship—sensed that Sam was everything he seemed to be. And more.

Alice stood and walked over to the balcony door. "What I *need* is a little fresh air and some company."

Kat grinned. Yes, just like Morgan, Alice had a flair for drama. "I don't imagine I'll have access to my room anytime soon. I'm happy to stay until then."

And she was. Even though she really wanted a shower and some clean clothes, she also didn't relish the idea of going back to her room alone just yet. Surely the incident in the atrium had been an accident, but she was still shaken by how close she'd come to losing her life. And she had to admit she'd like to get to know Alice a little better.

"Thanks," Sam said. "You should get some fresh air, too. You still look pale."

"I did nearly get crushed by a chandelier," she said, mimicking the words he'd used and trying to lighten the mood.

But Sam's expression darkened. "Glad you haven't forgotten."

A cold chill swept up Kat's nape, and her hand came up to press it away.

"Sammy, enough with your gloom and doom," Alice chided. "I hardly think she could forget what happened just thirty minutes ago."

Sam glanced at his grandmother and a sheepish expression softened his face. "Good," he said. "Hopefully, that will keep you both out of trouble while I'm gone."

His eyes held a teasing glint, and Kat's stomach flipped. She moved toward the phone and away from all the feelings he stirred up.

"We'll be fine," she said and picked up the phone to call the concierge station as Sam left the room. After the phone rang several times with no answer, Kat gave up for the time being. "I'll try again in a few minutes."

"You coming, then?" Alice asked as she stepped onto the balcony, then looked back at Kat. "Or maybe you'd like to freshen up first? It might feel good to splash some water on your face."

"I think I'll do that," Kat said. "I'll join you in a few minutes." She walked to the bathroom, her side aching where the scars stretched taut, shoulder bruised from rolling off the stage. Her gown was ruined, but that was the least of her concerns.

A deep shadow of unease swept in and stole the relief she'd felt earlier after escaping the chandelier. Could Sam's intuition be on the mark? What if someone had deliberately caused the explosion? She tried to push the thought away. Sam may be suspicious of her ex, but the idea of Max setting a bomb off was ludicrous to anyone who knew him. That wasn't the kind of fire he played with.

Regardless, Kat wanted to know what exactly had happened in the atrium. And she wanted off this ship before something else happened.

Days from land in every direction, she knew she was stuck.

She closed herself in the bathroom. The mirror glared

back at her in the bright fluorescent light and she winced as a headache flared. What a mess. Debris dotted her hair. Dust smudged her nose and her right cheek. Her eyes were bloodshot, burning from the too-familiar sting of smoke. Mascara smudged under her eyes. Hard to believe only an hour had passed since she'd left her cabin for her performance.

She sent up a silent prayer of thanks that she had survived, but she didn't feel relieved in the least. An eerie sense of danger crawled along her spine, dread pitting in her stomach. The opportunity to travel the world for the summer on a cruise ship had seemed like a gift—a chance to recharge and renew her spirits.

Sunshine. That was what Morgan had said. *You need lots of sunshine. And to put some distance between you and Max.*

It had worked, for a little while. Performing and sightseeing and experiencing the peace and relaxation of the open waters, Kat had begun to feel more like herself again. Over the past couple of days, though, alone in her room, the quiet had gotten to her. The sunshine she'd been hanging on to replaced with shadows of sadness from the past, and the enormity of what she'd be returning to at the end of the summer…a brand-new house, empty of everything that made it home.

The photos and videos. The scent of her father's cologne. The piano she'd woken up to Christmas morning when she was six years old.

Gone. All of it.

At least she had escaped.

Not your time to go. That was what her dad would have said. He'd believed that everything happened for a reason, and Kat had always believed that, too.

Lately, though, she'd begun to question. Her losses kept

stacking up, and she wasn't sure what else she had left to lose.

What purpose had her parents' deaths served? And why would God spare Kat's life but allow a fire to destroy her home—the home she'd grown up in—and with it all her tangible memories?

The questions swirled through her mind, but she had no answers. For now, she'd just have to clean up and be happy she could do it.

She turned on the faucet and washed her face, grateful for the warm water running over her chilled hands and rinsing the grime away. She pulled her hair out of its makeshift bun and finger combed it, then wet a hand towel, rubbing it along her arms and neck. She looked a little better, but still she stood, staring back at her herself. Willing herself not to think about what would have happened if Sam hadn't been in the atrium tonight. Forcing herself not to think about his questions, but, of course, she couldn't stop thinking about them.

Enemies? No one came to mind. She wasn't prone to conflict, never had been. Growing up as an only child had instilled in Kat a sense of peace and order that she'd carried with her into adulthood. She didn't like to make waves, and she tried not to hang around people who did. Life was too uncertain, she'd found, to allow anger and bitterness to fester.

Even after Max's betrayal, she tried not to let her emotions take control. Letting him go had been much easier than she'd expected. She realized that perhaps she'd been more in love with the idea of settling down and starting a family than she'd been in love with Max.

Now she wasn't sure what she wanted to do after her contract was up. There was a certain allure to the sea, but it was a short-term gig. She could go back to teaching at the university, or she could open a private piano studio.

She could take a year off and concentrate on composing music for a new CD. Nothing sounded enticing lately, and she hoped her path would become clear given a little more time.

"God is in control," she whispered at her reflection. She used to believe that. Even after her mother's death, Kat's trust in God had never wavered. Lately, though, she'd wondered.

Surely, He could have given her just a little more time with her father. Why bring her back home and draw her in deep only to take him away so soon?

At least you had some time with him. That was what Morgan had reminded her quietly, and Kat knew she was right. But it hurt. And now she was more alone than she'd ever been.

Watching Sam with his grandmother reminded her of what she was missing, what she'd been missing for most of her life. A real sense of family. People to share life with. Morgan was the closest thing she had to family now, and she was anxious to get back to her room so she could check on her.

A quiet tap sounded at the bathroom door. "Everything okay in there?" Alice called from the other side.

Kat opened the door. "Yes, thanks. I feel a lot better now."

Alice swept a quick glance over Kat and nodded. "Still in one piece, and all cleaned up. Too bad about the dress."

Kat stepped out into the room. "It was my favorite one. My dad bought it for me." And since the dress had been at the dry cleaner's the week of the fire, it had been one of the only things she had left of her father.

Through slurred speech that was painful to listen to, he'd apologized for missing out on so much, for being too absorbed in his own grief to help Kat through hers. Said he should have done the things a mother would have done, like taking her for manicures and buying her a prom dress. So he'd told her he wanted to buy her next concert gown. Morgan had gone with her, snapped photos of Kat in her favorite choices. Later, Kat had come home to show her father the pictures and ask his opinion.

He'd never see her in a wedding gown or walk her down the aisle, but she'd at least shared those moments with him and seen the love shimmering in his fading brown eyes.

The memory hit her suddenly and without warning, and she felt the heat of tears threaten. She walked to the chair and grabbed the blanket, facing away from Alice so she wouldn't see.

"Still chilly?" Alice said. "I got through to the concierge while you were in the bathroom, and they said they'd get your key to you soon."

"Oh, thank you. It'll be nice to change into some dry clothes."

"For sure. Come on out to the balcony with me. Knowing Sam, he'll be a while yet." She smiled, pride lighting her eyes. "He was born for the work he does. It's as if God gave him an extra little bit of bravery and honor. He's just…not your average young man. But I'm sure you noticed."

"He *was* the only one running toward me while the chandelier was coming down."

"Exactly!" Alice nodded as if they'd just agreed on some deep philosophical truth. "Now, let's sit down and try to enjoy this evening," she said cheerfully. "It isn't every day we face death straight on and live to tell about it."

Her words did anything but cheer Kat. She hadn't faced death once, but twice, and she didn't want to face it again anytime soon.

FOUR

The sharp scent of burned wiring stung Sam's nose as he made his way down the nearly empty stairway. He expected voices echoing up from the atrium, but the ship was eerily quiet. He hurried down the stairs, anxious for a good look at the scene, wanting to get a better feel for what had happened.

He hoped it was simply an electrical malfunction, but his gut told him otherwise. The timing had been too convenient—a lot of people had been streaming through the atrium while Kathryn performed and could have been taken out by the explosion. It was a hallmark of a terrorist act: injure as many people as possible. Ship security was tight, but criminals always managed to find a way.

An image of Kat flashed in his mind: the horror that washed over her face as the flames burst right above her.

He'd seen that same look on his wife's face many times in his nightmares. For months after the car accident, he saw those terror-stricken eyes whenever he turned out the lights. Had Marissa seen the broken-down truck at the last minute and known her life was about to end? If he'd cut out on work and come home just a day earlier, would she still be alive today? Would he be at home right now, playing with their two-year-old daughter?

He would never find the answers to satisfy his feelings

of guilt. Sam wasn't used to failing, and he didn't plan to make a habit of it. He would find answers for Kat, and he would make sure that she *and* his grandmother both made it safely off the ship and back home.

"Sir!" someone called, drawing Sam's thoughts back to the present. To the musty, smoke-filled air. To the broken bits of piano two floors down. To the two cruise employees who were moving up the stairs, heading straight for Sam.

Neither looked old enough to have graduated high school. The taller of the two caught up with Sam and attempted to stand in his way. Lanky and awkward, he wore a white uniform that was just a little short in the pants and arms.

"We've been asked to remind passengers to stay in their cabins until further notice," he said.

Sam narrowed his gaze and waited a beat. Watched the young men shift uncomfortably.

"Thank you for the reminder," he finally said. "But I don't intend to stay in my cabin."

"I'm afraid you don't have a choice." The second crew member joined the first, jogging up behind his coworker as if to offer moral and physical support.

He could offer whatever he wanted, but Sam would go where he desired.

"No?" He took a step closer, and the two exchanged worried glances. Sam didn't make a habit of physically intimidating people, but he towered over both kids and probably had fifty pounds of muscle on each of them. He doubted they'd attempt to detain him.

"It's for passenger safety," the second of the two said. Much shorter than his buddy, he had freckled skin and dark brown eyes behind round glasses. He pushed them higher up the bridge of his nose and shifted anxiously. "It should only be for a couple of hours."

"Look, you've done your job," Sam responded. "You've

warned me. I've decided to ignore you. If something happens, you can tell your boss and anyone who asks that you did your due diligence."

"But—" the freckle-faced kid began.

"Go ahead and let your boss know." Sam walked past them, ignoring the sputtered protests and unhappy shouts. They'd call Security, and he'd deal with that, too. He'd been hardwired from day one to be proactive. His parents said he'd always been a daredevil. His siblings said he was too independent for his own good. They were right, but he used both qualities to his advantage in his work.

In his personal life? Sometimes they got him into trouble. Sometimes they kept him from remembering important dates like birthdays and anniversaries. And 3-D sonogram pictures. Memories of his failures were never on short supply lately, hadn't been for the past two years. His work kept him from falling too deeply into a pattern of regret. With a job to do, there was simply no time to dwell on the past.

Two uniformed security officers and a firefighter met him as he turned onto the second flight of steps, their expressions hard. Unlike the kids who'd tried to stop him before, these three looked as if they meant business.

"Sir, you're going to have to return to your cabin," a bulky guy with a menacing demeanor said. His name badge said "Larsen," but he didn't bother to introduce himself. He stared hard at Sam, arms crossed, feet in a wide stance that was meant to intimidate. "We're investigating a fire that occurred in the lobby below," the man continued. "All passengers need to stay clear of the area for their own safety."

Sam pulled out his wallet. He didn't have his credentials, but he handed over a business card. "Sam West, Secret Service," he said. "I was there when the incident occurred. I think we all know it wasn't a simple fire."

"We don't know anything," the second officer said. A few years younger than Larsen and at least three inches taller, the officer looked fit and strong in his tailored uniform, his blond hair in a high fade cut. Sam pegged him as former military, and that might play to Sam's advantage. "I don't guess we need the Secret Service involved," the officer said. "We're trying to avoid contaminating evidence."

"Before the Secret Service, I worked for the Miami PD," Sam added. "I'm not trying to get in your way. I just figured the more hands, the better."

"Right." Larsen's eyes gleamed black with anger. No one liked other departments nosing in on their investigations. "I don't think we need any more hands. We've got things—"

"Actually—" the younger man cut him off "—it might not be a bad thing to have an extra set of eyes. I'm Nick Callahan. A good friend of mine works for the Miami PD—his name's Brent Mitchem." He held a hand out toward Sam, and they shook.

"Brent Mitchem, solid officer," Sam said. "Got to know him pretty well on the night shift a few years back."

"How 'bout that?" Nick said with a brief smile that didn't quite meet his eyes. Then it was gone, and he was all business again. "Been working cruises for nine years, and I've never seen anything like this before. Come on. I'll bring you down. Don't touch anything, though. We need to preserve the scene."

"Now, hold on a minute," Larsen said, face ruddy with agitation. "Policy—"

"Policy," Nick cut in, "should welcome an extra pair of eyes. We've got six thousand people on board with no way to evacuate." He looked pointedly at his partner. "Why don't you check on his creds? As long as they check out, and I'm sure they will, there's no reason to keep him in the dark about what's going on."

"You're the boss," Larsen muttered as he brushed past them, and Nick motioned toward the man next to him.

"This is Colton Hughes. He heads up our firefighting team."

"Nice to meet you." Sam offered a hand, appreciated the firefighter's firm grip and steady gaze.

"Appreciate your coming down," Hughes said as Nick finally began to lead the way down two more flights of stairs to the atrium.

Sam was anxious to get to the scene, observe what he could and return to the room to check on Grandma and Kathryn. He didn't want to leave them alone for long, especially Kat.

Back home, he'd have the discipline to keep his distance from a woman like Kat, the kind of woman whose smile alone could stir up dreams he hadn't entertained for two years. But here on the ship Sam felt he had a duty to stay close. At least that was what he tried to tell himself, even as Kathryn's liquid amber eyes flashed in his mind. He'd seen sadness there behind her easy sense of humor, and an inner strength that drew him in.

Sam denied the thought almost as soon as it rose, focusing instead on the atrium ahead as he and the other two men exited the stairwell on deck eight.

The smoke had cleared, leaving behind a gray film over every surface and an acrid scent Sam couldn't quite place. Shards of crystal lay heaped with splintered wood and twisted piano strings. Yellow tape cordoned off most of the atrium. Sam's gaze traveled straight up from the mess to the scorched opening in the ceiling.

"That's a lot of damage," he said. "Will we dock at the nearest port?"

"The closest port is where we're headed."

Sam had expected as much, but had hoped to hear otherwise. A week ago, they'd departed from São Paulo,

Brazil, making two other stops in the country before embarking on the next leg of their trip—a seven-night journey to the Canary Islands.

Impeccable timing, for sure, with three days left at sea before reaching their destination. The realization only fed his suspicion that it wasn't an accident that had caused the chandelier to fall.

"Any leads on what happened?"

Sam had expected to see a crew of officers combing through the debris for evidence, but he counted only three officers in the area other than Nick, and they stood outside the borders of the yellow tape.

Nick shook his head. "We don't have the means to perform a thorough investigation on a cruise ship. Our job is to preserve the scene until we dock."

Sam didn't like the sounds of that. With three days until they reached land, they needed to discover the origin of the explosion in the atrium before something worse happened.

"What about security footage?"

Nick pointed to a spot two decks above, parallel to where the chandelier had hung. "I've got men scrolling through footage from that camera specifically. Hopefully, we'll be able to get a closer view of how it all started."

"What are your initial thoughts on the cause?" Sam asked.

Nick was quiet for a moment, not taking his eyes off the wreckage. Finally, he gestured toward Colton. "Colton suggested it could have started with a bulb exploding. That could account for the popping sound many people heard."

"Is that a common malfunction?"

Colton shook his head. "Rare. And not likely to cause such a big fire."

"Could it have caused the chandelier to come down?" Sam pressed, because the theory didn't sit right with him.

"Not unless one exploded and caused several others to explode in succession."

"Is that possible?"

Colton nodded. "Sure. Anything's possible. Could also be faulty wiring. Ship's pretty new—this is only her second year at sea."

"So, we're talking a long shot." Sam peered up at the hole in the ceiling. "I'd say there was more to it than a few bulbs popping. Do you agree?"

Neither man seemed eager to share more, but Sam was sure they were all following the same line of thought. Someone had caused the chandelier to fall. Deliberately.

"Off the record," he assured them. "I'd be the last one to spread word that could incite panic."

Nick turned to Sam, a troubled expression in his eyes. "The most unlikely scenario, of course—it could have been a bomb."

Sam said nothing. The theory didn't surprise him. Several times he had replayed the sounds he'd heard, the loud pop, the explosion. And that chemical scent.

"Why unlikely?" Sam asked. In his opinion, a bomb was the most likely possibility.

"Our security policies are tighter than even air-travel policies. It'd be tough to get explosives on board," Nick said.

"Looks to me like someone may have figured out a way," Sam said. "You can't ignore the extent of the damage."

"Hard to believe the pianist made it out alive," Nick said. "You said you were there when it happened?"

"I was a few feet away."

Nick glanced at him, assessing. "Some witnesses said an unknown man pushed the pianist out of the way just before the chandelier came down. That you?"

"Yes."

"You see anything or hear anything before then?"

"Thought I did," Sam said. "Saw a man rushing through the crowd and into the coffee shop over there." He pointed in the direction of the shop. "Almost as soon as he was gone, I heard the loud pop, and the chandelier burst into flames."

"Did you get a good look at him?" Nick asked, eyes lit with interest.

"No. Just saw his back in a passing glimpse. Dark jacket, black ball cap, dark pants, maybe cargo-style."

Nick turned toward the coffee shop. "I'll have my team pay close attention to footage from that angle, too."

"Excuse me, I've got a briefing with my team," Colton said from behind them. "Callahan, we'll catch up later. Sam, good to meet you." He hurried back toward the steps and away from the accident scene.

"Any chance I can get a look at that security footage?" Sam asked, and Nick hesitated.

"Let me get back to you on that," he said. "I'll need you to verify the person you saw when we get ahold of the image. And I may ask for your assistance if I need more hands. If this was just an accident, that's one thing. If it wasn't…"

He let the thought trail off, but Sam knew where he was going.

If it wasn't, there could be more trouble to come, and days from land, they were in a vulnerable position. Getting six thousand people safely into lifeboats would be a nightmare. Sam had stood through the muster station drill before the cruise set out, and he'd listened as a fresh-out-of-high-school crew member instructed them on ship-evacuation procedures. As if everyone would simply follow the muster rules in the case of an emergency. Sam had spent nearly a decade in law enforcement, and he'd seen people in desperation. Knew one human truth: in times of disaster, most people cling to just one rule—every man for himself.

Black water stretched before them under a moonless sky. Dark clouds had rolled in, bringing a cool breeze. Kat tugged the blanket around her shoulders. She was chilled, but happier outside than in. Couldn't stand another minute breathing in the stench of smoke from her dress. At least out here, the breeze carried the odor away.

"Nothing as far as the eye can see. Just water and sky and stars. All of it a testimony to God's creative genius." Alice spoke the words softly. "I always wanted to go on a cruise with my Frank. I wish we'd had the chance."

"Frank?"

"My husband. He had an artist's soul and would have enjoyed every moment. It wasn't meant to be, though. He passed away a little over a year ago. We had booked this trip already. It was to be our fiftieth-anniversary celebration."

"I'm sorry." Words were never enough, but they were all Kat had. "This trip must be hard for you."

Alice watched the waves, silent for a moment. "I do wish he was here. But God's been good to me. Frank and I spent forty-nine wonderful years together, raised four children, became grandparents. We even got to be *great*-grandparents. Many people don't get that chance. I can't complain. Plus, Frank wouldn't have wanted me to come on this cruise and moon over the past."

"I'm sure it gets lonely, though, sometimes." Kat knew the feeling all too well.

"If I let it," Alice said. "Happily, I'm not alone on this cruise."

"Sam came with you."

"Sam. Yes." She sighed deeply. "My babysitter. He can

be a stick-in-the-mud, such a rule-follower. Always has
been. But my Red Hat Society ladies make up for it. Three
of them came, actually, to make sure I had a good time.
And let me tell you." She leaned close, eyes sparkling.
"We've been having a blast!"

"Does that mean you've been causing trouble?" Kat
asked, amused with Alice's sense of mischief.

"Causing it? Never! Trouble just seems to find me."

"So you really are a trouble magnet, Alice?"

"That's what my family says. All because of a few very
minor incidents. But let's not talk about that. Let's talk
about Sammy. He's a lot like my Frank."

"Is he?" Kat murmured, resistant to the turn in conversation. Alice clearly had an agenda that included finding a
woman for her grandson, and Kat didn't want to encourage
her. She'd learned at a young age to take care of herself,
and she'd done it well until Max had come along with his
charming words and pretty promises. She'd let herself start
dreaming then. What a mistake that had been.

"Oh, yes. He likes rules and quiet and *order*." She said
it as if it was a bad word, and Kat laughed.

"I like those things, too," she admitted.

Alice smiled. "But Sammy, he's got an edge to him,
too. His mom calls him her adrenaline junky."

"I guess that explains the Secret Service job."

"Yes. And he even looks the part," she said slyly. "Quite
a good-looking young man, isn't he?"

Kat laughed again, heat flushing her cheeks. *Good-
looking* wasn't the right term. Devastating. Yes, that was
the one. And Kat had experienced enough devastation for
one year. For a lifetime, really. "Very, and you're quite the
matchmaker, aren't you?"

"Guilty as charged." Alice smiled. "I can't help myself.
After nearly fifty years with the love of my life, I'm always
eager to see others find their perfect match."

"Nothing is perfect in this life," Kat responded, pushing back the image of Max as it rose in her mind. If he wasn't happy, he should have broken off their relationship. Instead, he got involved with another woman. *While* Kat was in the hospital. She didn't want him back, but the betrayal still burned.

"You're right, but there are some things that come very close. This moment, for one." Alice gestured to the broad expanse of dark ocean. "The soft sound of waves lapping against the ship. The dark swirl of clouds filling the night sky. Is that not close to perfect?"

Kat was cold, the sky looked dreary, and the clouds seemed a little foreboding. "I think your Frank wasn't the only one in the family with an artistic soul."

"You're right about that, dear. Maybe that's why we had such a wonderful marriage."

Someone knocked on the door before Kat could ask more questions about Alice and her husband, about the family that seemed almost too good to be true. For a while, her own family had seemed that way, too…but she'd learned that most things that were too good to be true simply didn't last.

"Sit tight, Kat," Alice said as she stood. "You've been through a big scare. And it does these bones good to move around."

"I'm ready to go inside anyway," Kat said, following behind as Alice answered the door.

"I have a keycard for Kathryn Brooks." Johann stood just outside the door, blond hair pulled back into a ponytail, a tight smile on his angular face. "May I do anything else for you ladies this evening?"

"Not unless you can break us out of this joint."

Kat laughed behind Alice, but Johann cocked his head, the joke lost in translation.

"Just a little joke," Alice said. "Actually, would it be too much trouble to get some tea brought up?"

Johann nodded and quickly headed back down the hall.

"I'm sure the cabin stewards are getting a run for their money right now with everyone trapped in their rooms," Alice said as she handed Kat her key. "Now, you go on down to your room and take that shower you've been waiting on."

Kat hesitated. As desperate as she was to get into her room, Sam wasn't back yet. "I told Sam I'd stay—"

"Actually, you didn't. You said you'd stay while you waited for your key. You did. Now, go on to your room, clean up and come back to share some tea with me. I guess my Red Hat friends are stuck in their rooms, too, and I get lonely without company."

Next thing Kat knew, she was out in the corridor, her keycard in hand, not quite sure how she'd gotten there. She considered knocking on Alice's door, but she was just relieved and more than ready to change out of the smoky, wet clothes.

The hall was silent and empty, unusual and eerie for eight in the evening on a cruise ship. She hurried along the teal carpet, unsettled by the quiet. She almost turned back. Everyone else was following the captain's instructions to stay in their rooms. Except her. But the promise of a hot shower was too enticing to pass up. She ignored the unnatural silence, the hairs rising at the nape of her neck. What had happened down in the atrium had been a freak accident, she was sure, and she wouldn't let it throw her into an anxiety attack.

Maybe cruising hadn't been the best idea, so soon after so much trauma. But the stint had seemed to come at the perfect time. She had needed desperately to get away. To find some solace. To regroup.

The hall seemed longer than it had been earlier. And

much emptier. Yet she had a haunting feeling she wasn't alone.

She glanced behind her. No one there. She quickened her steps, the quiet settling around her, eerie and thick. She looked back again. Hunted. That was how she felt, but she shook the thought away. She'd almost been killed a few hours ago, and she was probably still shaken from that.

Trust your instincts.

Wasn't that what every police officer who taught women's safety classes said? *Go with your gut. Listen to your instincts. When you think you're in danger, don't second-guess yourself.*

She shivered, quickening her pace even more, anxious to get to her cabin. Almost there. When she finally reached her door, Kat moved to swipe her keycard. But she sensed movement to her right. She peered down the hallway to where it darkened and veered left. Empty and quiet and lonely.

And then a shadowy figure emerged and sharp terror washed over her. She couldn't see his eyes behind the dark glasses he wore and the black cap he'd pulled low. But there was no mistaking his stride was aimed at her.

FIVE

Kat's hand shook as she swiped her keycard, desperate to get inside her room. The lock still blinked red! In her periphery, the man drew closer. Kat flipped the card, swiped again. There! She yanked down on the handle, swinging the door open, and then tossed another look down the hallway.

But whoever had been there was nowhere to be seen. She stepped quickly over the threshold, heart slamming inside her chest.

"Wait."

The voice came from behind her, and Kat gasped, turning with arms out to defend herself.

"Whoa." Sam's hands came up, gently grabbed Kat's forearms. "Didn't mean to scare you."

Kat looked past him, down the hall. "Where did you come from?" she asked.

Sam gestured back toward Alice's room. "I was heading to my grandmother's room and noticed you down here. Everything okay?"

"I don't know," Kat said. "I thought I saw someone. No, I *know* I saw someone."

"What do you mean?"

Kat pointed. "I was opening my door, and when I looked

up, someone appeared from around the corner. He was walking toward me. Fast."

Sam's eyes narrowed, concern drawing his brows together. "What did he look like?" he asked.

Kathryn shook her head. "He had on a black hat and was wearing sunglasses. I barely saw him. I was so desperate to get into my room." She glanced back down the hall, assuring herself that the man was gone. "I don't know where he went."

"Listen, Kathryn, come on back to my grandmother's room. We should report the incident to Security."

Kat stepped back out into the corridor with Sam and looked down the hall one more time before turning with him to go back to Alice's room.

"I should have stayed there in the first place," Kat said. "I never was much of a babysitter."

Sam flashed a quick grin and motioned for her to follow him. "No harm done," he said. When they reached Alice's room, he knocked and cracked the door open. "Grandma, you decent?"

"At my age, does it really matter?"

"It does to me!" Sam said, then turned to Kat. "You're not fired," he said.

Kat laughed quietly, despite the fear he still read in her eyes. It was a sweet sound that Sam wanted to hear again. He'd been missing out on laughter for a long time now. He'd settled into a groove at work, and he'd almost forgotten. Forgotten what it felt like to relax, to let go a little and stay in the moment.

"Sorry," Kat said, "I was ready to go back to my room, and Alice insisted she'd be fine."

"Don't worry about it," Sam said as he opened the door wider and gestured for her to enter ahead of him. "She has a way of getting what she wants."

"I gathered."

"My ears are still good, young man," Alice chastised from within the room. Her white hair was in disarray from the sea breeze, cheeks flushed from the fresh air. She set her journal and pen on the nightstand next to a picture frame she kept by her bed wherever she went. It was a photo from two Christmases ago, and by all rights it should have brought up happy memories, but Sam's heart pitched whenever he looked at it—a painful glimpse of his family when it was still whole. Grandpa Frank was still here. And Marissa. They'd just learned that their first child would be a girl.

"Sammy, let the poor girl get cleaned up already," his grandmother said, breaking into his thoughts. He looked at Kat. His grandmother was right. He should have been more sensitive.

"You do look miserable," he told Kat. "Let's call Security and then I'll walk you back to your stateroom."

Kat shook her head and grabbed the blanket she'd been using. "No hurry. I want to hear what you found out."

"Okay, just give me a minute here." After leaving messages both at the security desk and also on Nick's cell phone, Sam looked up to find his grandmother eyeing him with curiosity.

"What was that all about?"

"Kat saw someone suspicious when she was heading to her room," he said. "I want to report it, but sounds like Security's overrun with calls right now."

Grandma flicked a gaze over at Kat and then back to Sam. "What did he do?"

"Nothing," Kat said. "But I got the feeling he'd been watching me, and he was coming at me fast."

Grandma looked at Sam. "Did you see him?"

Sam shook his head.

"Maybe he turned back when he saw Sam coming down the hall," Kat suggested.

"And maybe you should go on back downstairs again," Grandma said to Sam. "It's easy to ignore a phone call—not so easy to ignore a person standing in your way."

Sound advice.

"But first," his grandmother said, "what did you dig up?"

"Not a whole lot," Sam told her. "There's a team poring through surveillance tapes as we speak. But so far, nothing. The fire-team lead thinks it may have been an electrical malfunction or even a problem with the bulbs in the chandelier."

"What do *you* think?" his grandmother asked.

Sam rubbed his neck. "I'm hoping that's the case, something simple that can be resolved and prevented from happening again."

"And if it's not?" His grandmother read him well, always had.

"I spoke with Nick Callahan, the head of Security. He isn't writing off the possibility of an explosive." He didn't want them overly worried, but they'd be safer armed with knowledge than shielded from it.

"A bomb?" Kat paled, hands clenched together in front of her.

"Maybe," he responded. "It's not information that's being given out to passengers. We need to keep this under wraps until we reach port. Otherwise…"

"Mass panic." Kat supplied the words as she sat down on the couch. Her hands dropped from where she held the blanket, and she began turning the gold band on her finger again. Long, slender fingers with not a hint of polish on her trimmed nails. Everything about her was delicate, but he sensed a strength in her that piqued his interest.

Sam nodded. Keeping Kat and Alice in the dark wouldn't do them any good. "There are more than four thousand passengers on board, almost two thousand crew."

"Six thousand people with nowhere to go," Grandma chimed in as she reached for her oversize red hat and put it on. "It's best if we all just act like everything is normal. Or as normal as it can be when a mad bomber might be on the loose."

"Let's not get melodramatic, Grandma," Sam cautioned. "We don't have any evidence that this was a bomb. It's all speculation. And I wouldn't go telling your friends, either."

"You know I won't, Sammy."

"If people knew, they might start taking their chances with lifeboats," said Kat.

Sam agreed. The conversation had come up among the security team, as well. Everyone would be safer if they kept the matter contained and didn't alert the passengers.

"I got a look at the security offices," he continued. "Nick has a team working through video footage, but the process is slow. Only twelve security officers on ship, and they've got a huge task ahead of them. This ship is like a floating city," he added. "Not sure why the industry doesn't treat it as such. For this many people, they should have a much larger armed police force on board."

"So, are we turning back?" Kat asked.

"Doesn't sound like it. We're too far out."

"I don't like the sounds of this." Grandma frowned, brows knit together. She'd been acting before, caught up in the excitement, but she was a smart lady. She'd started to grasp the gravity of their situation.

"Nick's team seems capable," Sam said. "I have a feeling they'll get to the bottom of this." He said the words more out of comfort for his grandmother than conviction. The team was too small, their capabilities too limited.

His grandmother moved toward the balcony, her gaze set on the inky black beyond. "How would someone get an explosive onto a ship in the first place?"

Sam shrugged. "Security's tight but not foolproof. Especially if the guy knows his way around the ship."

"A crew member?" Alice suggested, then cracked a smiled. "It's like one of those murder-mystery dinners."

"We've been cruising for a week," Kat pointed out. "Couldn't it be anyone who took some time walking the ship in the past few days?"

Sam nodded. "Could be," he said. "Or it could be something as simple as the fire chief speculated."

He didn't believe his own words for a minute. The sound, the smell, the way the explosion started all led him to believe someone had rigged a device on that chandelier. He'd guess the guy had used a blasting cap on a remote. Something that could do a lot of damage but not sink the ship. Maybe he wanted to wreak havoc but didn't want to have to abandon ship. A coward.

"Yes, but that's not what you believe," Grandma said. "Kathryn, you should stay with me tonight. That couch is a pullout."

"I think I'd rather—"

A low beeping sounded over the intercom system.

"Attention all crew and passengers. This is your captain speaking. Please be advised that the fire in the atrium has been extinguished, and the scene has been locked down until investigators are able to board the ship and determine the cause of the accident. As our security team continues to sweep the ship, we encourage all guests to remain in their staterooms until nine-thirty this evening. At that time, you will be free to roam decks fourteen and fifteen. We expect to reopen most other areas by morning. We appreciate your cooperation in this matter."

"Oh, good," Alice said. "At least we can get ourselves a late-night snack in a half hour. I'm just famished from all this excitement."

"How about I pick up some snacks in a bit and bring

them back to the room," Sam offered. He didn't like the idea of his grandmother wandering around with a crowd of other passengers so soon after the incident in the atrium.

Grandma huffed. "Really, Sammy, if it were up to you, I'd stay in this room until we reached the Canary Islands. I'm so glad we don't have to turn back—I've heard it's just beautiful there. Have you ever been, Kat?"

"No. This is all new to me. This is only my third time on a cruise."

"I hope you don't have to spend all your time working," Grandma said. "It would be a shame to miss out on all the sites."

"I get out a little," Kat said with smile. "The job isn't too demanding."

"You're an incredible pianist," Sam said. "You must practice hours a day."

Color crept up her cheeks. Did the compliment make her uncomfortable? Or did he?

"Thank you. I haven't been able to practice as much as I'd like. My teaching schedule has been pretty demanding."

"So this gig is more like a break for you than a job?" Sam asked, determined to understand what had pushed Kat to sign on as a cruise ship entertainer.

"Something like that."

"And something *not* like that?" he prodded.

"It's a long story," Kat said.

"Sammy and I love long stories, don't we?"

No. Sam didn't usually appreciate lengthy stories. He liked people to answer his questions clearly and succinctly. But he wanted to hear Kat's long story.

When she didn't answer immediately, Grandma piped up. "I suspect I know what happened." Her voice hushed to a conspiratorial whisper as if she'd just had a revelation.

"She left home to get away from Max…oh, yes! That's what I would do, if I were—how old are you, Kat?"

Kat blinked. "Twenty-six."

"Yes, exactly. If I were twenty-six and in your shoes, I would take a job like this, too…set sail to find someone new, someone who would make me forget the—"

"No," Kat interrupted, an amused smile on her lips. He liked that she got his grandmother. Alice's humor didn't always go over so well. "I certainly didn't set sail looking for romance."

She blushed a deeper pink, and Sam thought that something his grandmother had said must have rung true. *Had* she been trying to get away from Max?

Kat shivered again, and Sam knew he should stop pushing for now. "You're freezing. Let me walk you back to your room."

"Thank you," she said, unwrapping the blanket from her shoulders and laying it on the back of a chair. He saw relief in her acceptance, knew she dreaded walking the hallway alone again. Someone had been stalking her in the corridor, and that knowledge only fed Sam's suspicion that the incident in the atrium had been triggered for a purpose, and that the purpose somehow involved Kathryn Brooks.

"Don't forget to come back, Kathryn," his grandmother called out, a twinkle in her eye. "I don't know where Johann is with our tea, but I'm going to call and find out."

"I'll be back," Kat agreed, opening the door.

Sam took her arm, leading her down the corridor. The woman needed to eat. Meat and potatoes. Cheesecake. Milk shakes.

He was tempted to tell her, but growing up with four sisters had taught him better. "Thanks for staying with my grandmother earlier. I know I was gone awhile."

"It wasn't exactly a chore," Kat said. "She's easy to be

around. I should have stayed longer—I know she wanted the company."

"Don't let her fool you. As soon as you walked out, she probably starting texting the family about what happened tonight."

"She texts?"

"And tweets. She also does competitive ballroom dancing and enjoys skydiving."

"No way." Kat laughed.

"All true."

"I think I want to be your grandmother when I grow up," Kat said, grinning, "But I don't think I'd ever skydive." She slid the card to open her door. "Thanks for walking me back."

"Not a problem. Call down to my grandmother's room when you're ready, and I'll come get you. And make sure you lock up."

"I will," she agreed. "I'll only be about twenty minutes."

She closed the door and Sam headed back to his grandmother's room, but his mind was on Kat. She had a gentleness about her and a sense of calm that was like a balm to his heightened energy.

The thought slowed his steps. He'd barely noticed another woman since Marissa had died, and guilt snagged at his conscience.

The guilt that wouldn't release its grip, two years steady. Sam had always been fiercely loyal. When he'd said *until death do us part*, he had meant forever. He'd kept himself busy since Marissa's death, and he liked it that way. Too busy to notice other women. The cruise had forced him to slow down, and he suspected Grandma had known it would.

He didn't like it. The extra time on his hands to think

about what he was missing. The slow moments to notice Kat's profile, the sweet curve of her lips.

He'd let his job interfere with his family, and Marissa had died because he hadn't been there.

He'd already proven that he couldn't give his all to his career and still have enough left for a family. Nothing had changed, he reminded himself.

Finally. Kat could grab a quick shower and put on something dry. She couldn't get rid of the cold feeling all over. She headed across the room to grab a change of clothes, but the blinking light on the telephone stopped her.

She hurried over to it, picked up the receiver. It must be Morgan. She dialed the access code and listened. The message had come in more than an hour ago. But the voice she heard was not her friend's.

"Hello, this is Lillian Foster. I hope I've been transferred to the correct room. I'm trying to reach my daughter, Morgan. Morgan, if you get this message, please call me as soon as you can." A pause, and then, "I love you. Call me. Bye now."

Kat saved the message and set the receiver down, anxiety churning in the pit of her stomach. Why was Lillian calling the ship looking for Morgan four days after she was supposed to have headed home? Hadn't Morgan told her mom she was on her way?

She thought back to the day Morgan had left. Kat had been heading toward the theater, on her way to rehearse for a performance that was due to start soon after the ship left port. She'd intended to take a detour by the gift shops on the way to set a time for dinner with Morgan. But as Kat moved to step off the elevator, Morgan had stepped on.

No, she hadn't stepped inside. She'd burst inside, eyes wide, a stricken look on her face.

She'd looked terrified.

The memory hit Kat hard. Almost as soon as Morgan had locked eyes with Kat, the look in her eyes had disappeared. She'd starting crying, told Kat that Jake was really sick.

"I need to go home. Now. It's really bad this time."

Kat had ridden back up to the twelfth deck with her best friend, walked to their room with her. Put her arm around her friend's shoulder. But when they'd gotten to their room, Morgan had pulled away from Kat's hug, avoiding eye contact as she opened the door. She wasn't acting like herself, Kat knew. But grief did that to a person. Morgan and her brother had always been close.

"Let me help you, Morgan. Just take what you need, and I'll take care of the rest."

"I'll be okay," Morgan said. *"You go on to your concert. There's not a lot of time."*

She'd been right. Kat wished she hadn't been. She'd wanted to help somehow, but Morgan needed to pack up, and Kat needed to run through her program before the theater doors opened. She'd hugged Morgan one more time, whispered a prayer for Jake and hurried down to the theater. Two hours later, the ship had set sail, and Kat's best friend was gone.

Kat now dug in her purse for her cell phone. She dialed Morgan's number, but the call went straight to voice mail, again. She left a message, knowing she sounded much more concerned than she should be. Any number of things could have happened. Morgan may have had a hard time getting a flight out, she could have lost her cell phone or she could be stuck on a long layover.

But four days was a long time. And Mrs. Foster's confused voice mail didn't match up with what Kat knew.

She scrolled down her address book for the number and dialed Morgan's mom.

There wasn't any answer at the Fosters' house.

"Great." Lillian had a cell phone that Morgan insisted she keep for emergencies, but Kat didn't have the number. She opened the drawers Morgan had been using. She'd left some of her things there; maybe she could find it.

Or she could call down to Security. They'd probably have access to Morgan's emergency contact information. She started back to the phone, and the room plunged into darkness.

Kat froze.

A power failure? Just in this wing or on the whole ship?

Her pulse jumped at the thought of a cruise ship losing power in the middle of the ocean. *Calm down,* she told herself. *Everything's fine. They have emergency generators for this kind of situation.*

The room was pitch-black and empty, but she had the icy feeling that she wasn't alone.

Stop it, she told herself. *You are twenty-six years old.* And she'd been sleeping with the lights on for as long as she could remember.

Maybe it was just the overhead light. Goose bumps rose on her arms, and Kat used the dim light from her phone to guide her way to the lamp switch over the bed, heart pounding furiously in her ears. She flipped the switch. Nothing.

She couldn't stay here, not with the darkness closing in around her. She'd go back down to Alice's room; maybe they had power.

She felt her way around the bed and started for the door, but an image of the man in the hallway flashed through her mind, and she hesitated. Maybe it was safer in here than out there. Any minute now, the lights would flicker back on.

She drew in a shaky breath and sat on the edge of the bed just as a sliding noise cut through the silence.

Kat jumped up. Her balcony door! Opening?

Fear exploded through her and Kat ran blindly, heart pounding with terror, footsteps closing in behind her.

SIX

A scream echoed from the hallway.

Loud, terrified.

Female.

Sam lunged toward the door in the darkness, his grandmother close at his heels. He waved her back. "You stay right here."

He swiftly unlocked the door and charged into the hallway.

Pitch-black. The lights had gone off in the whole wing. Kat's room was to the left, and he ran that way. Reaching into his pocket, he pulled out his cell phone. At home he always carried a set of keys with a flashlight, but this would have to do.

He shone the light in front of him, the glow barely piercing the darkness. He couldn't see. The scream came again, and adrenaline tore through him.

"Hello?" he called as he ran, heart pumping with urgency. "Kat?"

"Sam?" Kat emerged from the shadows, running, eyes wide with fear. He aimed the light beyond her. There. In the distance. A figure moving quickly. He strained to see, but the shadow disappeared. They were alone. But Sam wasn't convinced they had been.

He cupped Kat's elbow and steered her toward his grandmother's room. "What happened? Are you okay?"

"Someone was in my room," Kat whispered, breathless and shaken. "My balcony door opened, and he came at me." She shot a look over her shoulder. "What's going on?"

"I'm not sure," Sam said. "Come on, let's go back to my grandmother's room. I'll find a way to get through to Nick. And I think you should stay. I'll make up the couch for you."

"I think I'll take you up on that. Just for tonight."

He was surprised when she agreed. He knew he had no right to push her to share his grandmother's room. They were complete strangers, after all. But someone had broken into her room, had been waiting for her. Who? The same person who had been watching her in the hallway earlier? And what was his goal? Sam should have entered ahead of her, done a check of her room.

He pounded on the door. "Grandma, it's Sam!"

The door flew open, and his grandmother stepped back to let them in. "Was that you out there?" she asked. "What on earth happened?"

"Someone was in Kat's room," Sam said. He shut the door firmly behind them, secured the locks. "Grandma, open your laptop and get a little light in here. I'm calling Nick Callahan."

He dialed Nick's cell phone, praying he would pick up.

"Everything okay up there?" Nick said when he answered the phone. "Our lines are ringing over a power failure on deck twelve and a report of someone screaming. I'm almost there."

"It was Kathryn Brooks. Someone was in her room. Entered through the balcony. We're in room 1237." He ended the call, turned to his grandmother and Kat. The blue screen from Alice's laptop glowed on their faces. Grandma was unusually quiet as she sat on the edge of the bed.

"Nick's on his way up," he said. "Kathryn's staying here for the night," he added.

A tap sounded at the door. "Nick Callahan," the voice called from the other side of the door. Sam opened it.

Nick stepped inside, another officer waiting just outside in the shadows of the corridor.

Nick's gaze skimmed over Kat and caught on Sam, an unspoken communication passing between the two, then he extended a hand to Kat. "A pleasure to meet you, Ms. Brooks, though I'm sorry for the circumstances," he said. "I planned to meet with you shortly about the incident in the atrium, but it sounds like you've run into more trouble. Tell me what happened." His smile was kind, but his stance was alert and tense. Good. Sam could tell Nick was a leader, and he liked that.

"I was just about to call down to Security to try to get ahold of a phone number I needed. That's when the lights went out. I heard my balcony door sliding open and I ran. Whoever was in my room chased me. He would have caught up with me, but then Sam called out, and the guy ran in the other direction."

Nick looked at Sam, who nodded. "The lights went out here, and a minute later, we heard a scream. I ran into the hallway and found Kat. I tried to see with the light from my cell phone. Caught a glimpse of someone in the distance, but not enough to make out details."

Suddenly, the hall lights flickered on, and the corridor and the stateroom were bathed in bright fluorescent again. Nick's radio beeped. "A breaker switch, sir" came the voice on the other end. "Issue resolved."

"How does that happen?" Sam asked, not sure he bought into the explanation.

Officer Larsen stepped into the room from where he'd been stationed in the hall. "This kind of thing happens now and then on newer ships. Little kinks that need to be worked out."

"I'd say that's more than a little kink," Grandma noted. "And if that chandelier accident was a result of a little kink, too, then who knows what will happen next."

"I'm sorry for the scare you had," Nick offered. "Hopefully this is the last of it." He focused on Kat again. "You said you heard the balcony door open. Did you see anyone?"

"No. I *felt* like someone was there, I heard movement, footsteps." Then she added doubtfully, "Then again, I've never been comfortable in the dark."

"I saw someone in the hallway," Sam reminded her.

Nick thought for a minute, then quirked an eyebrow up. "He was farther down the hall, right? Someone else could have been in the hallway going to their room when the lights went out. Maybe you both panicked."

He had a point there, Sam had to agree.

"I wouldn't write it off, though," Sam said. "Not sure if you got my message, but about thirty minutes ago, Kat saw someone suspicious coming toward her in the hallway."

Nick looked at Kat, who recounted what had happened earlier.

"Let's go down to your room together and take a look," Nick offered when she'd finished. "See if anything seems out of place."

Sam followed Kat out into the hall as she led Nick and Larsen down to her stateroom.

"Let me have your keycard."

Kat passed it to Sam without question. He swiped the card and opened the door, entering ahead of her. She stepped just inside and waited by the door while the officers and Sam looked around.

Everything looked as it had when she'd entered earlier.

The towel monkey still hung from the ceiling, the curtains by the balcony were still closed.

"Balcony's secure," Sam said from behind the curtains. He stepped out.

"Anything seem out of place?" Nick asked Kat. She shook her head. No, nothing did. Had she imagined the whole thing? Surely the intruder hadn't taken the time to close and lock the door before chasing her.

"After the chandelier incident from earlier, I don't think we should take any chances," Sam said to Nick. "Can you post a guard outside her door?"

Nick gestured to the other officer. "This is Officer Tom Larsen," he said to Kat. "He'll stick around for a couple hours in this hallway, at least until I can review the security footage." Larsen said nothing, didn't even offer a hint of a smile. He looked grim and formidable, bald head and thick muscles.

Nick looked at Kat, apologetic. "I understand you were scared, Ms. Brooks, but I'd venture to guess you're a little on edge after what you experienced earlier tonight. It seems to me all of this could have been a product of that stress and fear."

"You may be right," she said, but she didn't believe it. Was her testimony not evidence enough?

"She'll be staying in 1237, my grandmother's room," Sam said.

"Do you feel comfortable with that, Ms. Brooks?" Nick asked.

She nodded. "Seems like the safest option. And you can just call me Kat."

"You go ahead and get settled, then. We'll update you in the morning."

Kat detected a hint of a Southern accent and immediately trusted Nick. He reminded her of visits to her uncle's ranch in West Virginia every summer—of homemade pies and catching fireflies at dusk. She'd stayed with her aunt and uncle for three consecutive summers after her mother died. They'd never had any children, and she seemed to fill a void in their life the same way they filled the one in hers.

"Sure," she said. "Just name a time. My calendar isn't exactly full."

Nick chuckled, crow's-feet crinkling at the corners of his eyes. "I'll give you a ring, then." He started to turn, but Kat didn't want to miss her opportunity.

"I know you're busy," she said, "but I wondered if you could help me get ahold of that information I was trying to track down before the lights went out tonight."

"What are you looking for?"

"My friend Morgan Foster got off the ship at the last port, and I haven't been able to get in touch with her since," she explained. "She works on the ship, and we've been rooming together. Her mother called and left a message looking for her, but she wasn't answering at home. I wanted to try to track down Mrs. Foster's cell-phone number."

"Why'd Morgan leave the ship?"

"A family emergency. I just want to make sure she's okay."

"I'll see what I can do," Nick said. "But it probably won't be until later tomorrow."

"I understand. Thank you."

Sam opened the door for the officers to depart, then cast a glance at Kat.

"Do you want to grab some of your things?" he asked.

"Good idea." Quickly, Kat set about packing a small bag. She grabbed some clothes along with her toothbrush and makeup and tucked everything into the bag, hands unsteady as she zipped them in. Someone had been on her balcony. She was almost sure of it. But where did he go? And how did he get back in to lock the balcony door? She was beginning to doubt herself.

But Sam had seen someone, too.

A cold chill had worked its way through her, and she grabbed a purple hoodie off the edge of the chair and pulled it on. She reached down to unplug her laptop so she could bring it, too.

"How you holding up?" Sam asked, a hand coming to her back. He rubbed the small of her back in a slow circle, and warmth spiraled through her.

"I'm okay." But she wasn't. Something dangerous was on this ship, and she wanted off. "Starting to think maybe I *should* take my chances with a lifeboat." Kat was only half-joking.

Everything had been perfectly fine, and then suddenly she'd almost been killed, and someone had tried to attack her in her room. Not to mention, she hadn't heard from Morgan in days—where *was* she? She needed to call Mrs. Foster as soon as she got to Alice's room.

"We're still safer here than out there," Sam said with a grim smile, then grabbed the handle of Kat's suitcase and led the way from her cabin down the hall.

Alice was on her room phone when they reentered. She waved to them. "Oh, yes, it was terrifying," she was saying. "We heard the scream, and it just sent chills up and down my body!"

Speaking of chills, Kat was determined to change. She was grimy, exhausted and cold to the bone. "Do you think she'll mind if I grab a shower?"

"Help yourself," Sam said and pulled her suitcase into the bathroom for her, stepping out. "I'll get the couch set up for you."

Kat closed herself in and pulled out her cell phone. Nothing yet. She hadn't expected anything, but she'd hoped.

She took a quick shower, then changed into khaki capris and a white long-sleeved T-shirt. The pajamas she'd brought wouldn't work with Sam in the room. All the while, the knot of anxiety twisted in her gut. Morgan wasn't just her friend. She was a sister-of-the-heart, the closest thing to family Kat had left.

She towel-dried her hair and combed it out, then let it be. She didn't have the energy to blow-dry her hair tonight, but she was glad to at least have gotten rid of the smell of smoke.

She stepped out of the bathroom, and a soft snore sounded from across the room. Kat caught Sam's eye and grinned.

Sam laughed quietly. "Come ten o'clock, no matter the time zone, Grandma's out. You look better."

He was leaning against the wall near the balcony, arms crossed over his chest, an appreciative gaze on Kat. Her breath caught at the soft look in his eyes. He looked like a hero in one of the romance novels Morgan was always reading. If she were here, she'd be swooning.

But she wasn't. Kat eyed the phone. Wondered if it would wake Alice if she made a phone call.

"Something wrong?" Sam asked.

He knew something was wrong, and he suspected it went beyond the creep lurking on Kat's balcony and the close call with the chandelier.

"Yes…maybe," she said. "Or maybe after everything that's happened, I'm just getting a little paranoid."

"About?"

"My friend. I'm really worried about her."

"Is she normally good at keeping in touch?" he asked. He tried to keep his tone neutral, but he'd wanted to broach the subject since Kat first told Nick about it. Was it coincidence that someone had just been in Kat's room, and her friend was missing? He didn't believe in coincidence, never had.

"She's great about it. We've been friends since the third grade, and nothing like this has ever happened before."

"That's a little concerning. But there are plenty of explanations. She could have lost her cell phone, may not have been able to get on a flight—"

"I know," Kat cut in softly. "I'm just worried."

"Try not to worry until we have all the facts."

"I'd like to call again, but I don't want to wake your grandmother. I should probably just wait until morning."

"You can call from my room," Sam suggested. "I know if it were my friend, I wouldn't be able to sleep until I'd done everything I could. Hold on."

He walked over to his grandmother, slid her journal out from under her hands and set it on the nightstand next to her Bible. Then he slipped off her red flats and set them by the wall.

Kat moved to the closet and pulled out an extra blanket. "Here," she whispered and moved to help him lay the blanket on Alice. It was something Sam had done dozens of times, but watching Kathryn do it did something to his heart. Maybe because Grandma seemed just a little more fragile than she'd been before Grandpa Frank died. Maybe because he knew that the time would come when she would need more help.

Maybe because Kat looked lovely, her hair drying in shiny waves down her back, the dim light casting a warm glow on her skin.

He glanced away and his eyes caught on the Bible again. An image flashed in Sam's memory. From two decades past. New to the family, enfolded in a love he'd never experienced and wasn't sure how to accept.

"I have something for you," his new grandmother said. She pulled a thick leather-bound book from the edge of

*the top shelf. "When each of my grandchildren turns ten,
I present a Bible. Well, you're eleven, but it's not too late.
You're my grandchild, and I want you to have this."*

*She walked over and offered it to him. He grasped the
binding with both hands, the leather cool against damp
palms. Traced a finger over his name engraved on the bottom front cover. Samuel Michael Jones West.*

*He looked up at her, noticed the glistening sheen in
her eyes. She nodded. "Doesn't matter to us if your birth
certificate ever has our last name. In our hearts we are
a family, and God puts families together. Hold on to that,
son. Every answer you'll ever need is between those two
covers you're holding in your hands."*

His grandmother had only ever spoken truth, but Sam
had read the Bible cover to cover many times, and twenty
years after that first day in his home, he still had more
questions than answers. Even so, he offered up a silent
prayer of protection over the ship, his grandmother and Kat.

SEVEN

"You ready?" Sam asked. Kat nodded and followed him to his stateroom. She'd make the phone call and get out. She was a logical person, not prone to dreaming. But even she could look at the facts and know that her attraction for Sam was blooming. She'd read about this before, though. Where bonding happened during a traumatic event. Not a good foundation for a relationship, not that he was offering her one.

She dialed Morgan's home number once more. It had only been an hour, so it wasn't surprising that Mrs. Foster wasn't home. She was probably staying at the hospital with Jake. If she couldn't get ahold of her tonight, maybe tomorrow she'd start calling local hospitals. They'd always gone to Jackson Memorial or South Miami.

She pressed End Call as soon as the answering machine picked up. "She's still not answering. But thanks for letting me make the call."

"You know, maybe if you called down to Human Resources they could help you out sooner than Nick will get to you."

"I don't know why I didn't think of that earlier," Kat said. "I doubt anyone will be in the office, but I'll see." She moved to the phone on the desk and dialed the operator, waited to be transferred.

Her hopes sank when yet another answering machine clicked on, but she waited on the line and left a message anyway. She set the phone in its receiver with more force than she'd intended.

"No success, I take it?" Sam asked.

"No." She sighed. "I need to do *something*."

"Do you know Mrs. Foster's address?"

"Yes, Morgan lives there when she's not working."

"I may be able to help you." Sam reached over and grabbed a memo pad, handed it to Kat with a pen. "Jot down her information. Name. Home address. Phone number. I'll make some calls."

"Really?" Kat pulled her cell phone out and scrolled through her list of contacts. She copied down the information Sam had asked for, trying not to get her hopes up too high. "Do you think you can sweet-talk some urgency into Nick?"

"Not hardly." He smiled as he took the paper, his eyes a deep gray that made her think of dusky spring skies. "But I have a brother with the Miami Police Department. He might be able to pull some strings."

She wanted to hug him. She really did.

"I appreciate it. Thank you. I put my number there, too."

"I'm not sure of the time back in Florida," Sam said, reaching for his cell phone. "I may not reach my brother tonight."

She nodded. "I understand."

His gaze lingered for just a moment. "Is there a story behind the ring?"

She looked down at her hands, at the gold band on her finger. She was doing it again. A nervous habit.

"It was my mother's wedding band. She died when I was twelve. A brain tumor. My dad had it sized for me for my sixteenth birthday."

"I'm sorry. You've been through a lot."

She looked down at the ring. "It's been a long time."

"Some people say time heals, but that's not the case, in my experience."

She looked up at him then as he scrolled through a list on his cell phone. "Time soothes, but it doesn't heal."

"I've discovered that, too," Sam said quietly as he put the phone to his ear. Dark lashes hooded his eyes, but Kat was sure she'd seen something there. A pressing, aching sadness, and she wondered what had caused it in Sam's life.

Sam pushed back the memories of loss and failure, listening impatiently to the ringtone in his ear. He didn't even know Morgan, wasn't too concerned about her whereabouts. Not yet, anyway. But calling in some favors kept him busy, and right now, he needed to keep busy.

Sitting still wasn't in his makeup. He needed a job to do. He itched to be in the thick of the investigation on ship, but despite Nick allowing Sam into the security office, he knew he was an outsider and could expect to be treated like one.

He clenched his fists, frustrated. Lacking information made his job much more difficult. But he'd successfully protected many people in his life with very little solid information on the threats they were up against.

He hadn't been there for Marissa when she was in the accident. But he was here now, with his grandmother. With Kat. And he would protect them with everything he had. He wouldn't fail. Not this time.

His brother's voice mail picked up, and Sam waited to leave a message. It was the best he could do, but he wished he could do more.

But just as the recording beep sounded, another call came through. Cody. He'd always been able to count on his only brother. Sam switched over to connect.

"Sam, I saw you calling but couldn't get to the phone in time. Everything okay?"

"For now, at least," Sam said. "Grandma's enjoying herself," he added to reassure his older brother.

"But?"

"Something's not quite right on this ship, Cody," Sam began, and he filled his brother in on all that had transpired. He watched Kathryn in his periphery, caught her zip up the purple hoodie she wore, noticed her arms folding tighter across her chest as she listened. Her fear was palpable, and he couldn't blame her. They had a strong disadvantage in the middle of the ocean with no way to escape.

His brother let out a low whistle when Sam finished. "Haven't seen anything come up on the news yet. What can I do?"

"For Grandma and me, not much," Sam told him. "Just fill in the family and ask them to pray for safety. But the pianist, Kathryn, could use some help. Her roommate left the ship a few days ago and no one's heard from her since. Kathryn's trying to get ahold of her friend's mother but can't track down her cell-phone number."

"I'll see what I can do," Cody said. "Anything else I need to know about this pianist named Kathryn?"

Sam detected the good-natured tease in his brother's voice and looked over at Kat again. If she wasn't in the room with him, he might be tempted to confide in his brother. "That's it," he said instead.

"Hmm. Okay, well, I'm heading out the door, but you can email me the information. I'm on nights this week, so I'll get to it in a few hours. Soon enough?"

It would have to be. "Thanks, Cody."

"Sure, but listen—keep me posted on what's going on. I don't like the sounds of the situation out there."

"I'll check in with you tomorrow."

"Okay, stay safe."

He disconnected and took a seat on the couch. "He'll work on it for me tonight," he told her.

"Thank you," Kat said. "It sounds like you have a really close family. Tell me about them." Longing shone in her eyes, and Sam sensed she wanted to stay for a while.

"We are close," he agreed. "And sometimes loud. In each other's business." He grinned. "People who never give up on each other."

"Sounds like the kind of family I wanted when I was growing up."

"That's because you were never one of six siblings sharing a lone bathroom." He laughed. "Four sisters and a brother. I came into the picture later. I was eleven years old when my parents brought me home."

"You were adopted?"

"Fostered first. I thought it was just going to be another placement, but it stuck. My parents were really good at taking the tough-case kids and making them feel loved."

"Wow, that's incredible," she said. "Are you the youngest, then?"

"No, Emily is—she's in college. She joined our family when she was fifteen and pregnant. She and her son, Parker, still live at home with our parents. Next are Jules and Leah—they're twins. Not identical, though. Meg is the oldest of my sisters. She's a year younger than I am. Cody's the oldest of the pack."

"So were you and your brother always close?"

Sam nodded. "Since day one. Cody's two years older, but he always included me whenever he was hanging out with friends or riding his bike down to the corner store. Our mom always said that with so many girls in the house, we'd have to stick together."

They had. Cody was dependable, and he'd never failed Sam yet. Sam was reasonably sure he'd have Lillian Foster's number in hand before Kat woke up in the morning.

Kat had pulled her feet up onto the chair, arms wrapped around her shins, chin resting on her knees.

"But let's get back to you. Why did you really take this job, Kat?"

Alice was right. Sam was like a dog with a bone. She could simply tell him she didn't want to talk about it, but she wouldn't. Because something about the way he asked her this time, the way he watched her expectantly, hopefully, told her he really cared. That he was a safe person to confide in.

He leaned forward on the couch, waiting for Kat to answer.

"Is this confession time, then?" she asked.

"Do you have something to confess?" He looked back at her, eyes dark, and she couldn't read his expression.

Yes. That all she really wanted to do was sit on the couch next to him, lean her head against him and not talk at all.

Ridiculous, she chided herself. *You barely know the man.* Then why did she feel like she did? Like if she sidled up next to him on that couch right now, he would simply set an arm around her shoulders as if it was exactly where she was meant to be?

Instead, she stayed.

"It's not a confession, just hard to explain, I guess. So I avoid it."

He waited, and she knew that was what he was good at. He'd probably taken a hundred courses on interviewing and getting subjects to talk. It was working on her.

"After my dad died, I stayed in his house for a bit. I was going to finish out the year teaching and then decide whether to start performing again. There was a fire, destroyed the whole house. I almost didn't make it out."

"That's terrible. What happened?"

"I fell asleep reading. I do that a lot. Woke up at three in the morning. There was fire everywhere."

Her pulse raced as the images came back to her, the bright flames, the hot, hot heat and cloying, stinging smoke.

"I was on the second floor. Couldn't get to my window. The only way out was to make a run for it, right through the fire. I remember just chanting a prayer that God would save me."

"Brave. A lot of people in that same situation wouldn't make it out. The pain would be too intense."

"The aftermath was much more painful than the actual burns."

Something flickered in his eyes, but almost as soon as she'd seen it, it was gone.

"What caused the fire?"

"The lamp cord was damaged. I didn't know because the cord ran under the throw rug in the room."

Sam let out a breath, shook his head. "Did you end up in the hospital?"

She nodded, a hand absently running over the top of her left thigh. "Mostly second-degree burns on my left leg, up to my ribs. I was there about three weeks."

"And when you got out of the hospital, you had nowhere to go?"

Kat's eyes stung, but she held the tears at bay. It wasn't exactly true. Morgan's mom had invited her to stay with them for a while, but she hadn't wanted to impose. Her aunt and uncle said their doors were always open, but she'd have to relocate. "When I got out of the hospital, I had to deal with insurance and builders. I leased an apartment for the short-term. The new house should be ready by the time my contract is up. That was part of the reason for taking the job. It was good timing."

"And the other reason?" Sam prodded. "Max?"

"Max was a very small part. He wouldn't leave me alone, kept showing up at the college, leaving notes on my car. I was still recovering and having to deal with the house and my dad's estate... It was all too much."

"Why'd you break up?"

Kat shifted in the chair. The last thing she wanted to discuss with Sam was her relationship with Max. She shrugged, attempting to look unfettered by what had happened. "It was a long time in coming. But the nail in the coffin was that while I was in the hospital back in April, Morgan caught him cheating."

Sam raised an eyebrow. "For someone who cheated, he seems awfully determined to win you back."

"He wants what he can't have. When he gets it, he wants something else."

"So he can't have you, and he follows you onto this cruise, hoping to win you back." Sam shook his head. "That's not normal, Kat."

She supposed it wasn't but shrugged. She didn't want to keep talking about Max.

"So, that's it?" Sam asked. "You just wanted to get away from everything."

She grinned. "Not sure how well that worked out, all things considered."

"It worked out for me, anyway," he said, and there was no mistaking the glint in his eye. Kat's heart skipped a beat; she thought he might say more.

He brushed a hand through his hair, then stood. "You look exhausted. Let's get you back to my grandmother's room so you can get some sleep."

She followed him to the door, footsteps heavy with reluctance. She told herself it was because she didn't want to be alone, not after what had transpired in the past few hours. There was some truth there. Even though Alice was in the room, Kat didn't want to face the dark. But something far more powerful than fear beckoned her to stay. She felt safe with Sam. Absurd, since she'd only known him for a few hours. But there it was. Safe and cared for. It had been a long time since anyone had taken care of her. Too long.

"Hold on a minute," Sam said. He turned back. "Let me give you my number."

He grabbed the notepad off the desk, scribbled down his information and handed it to Kat. "This is my cell. Call me if you need anything."

"Thank you for everything you've done for me," Kat said.

"You act like we're already saying goodbye," he said with the kind of smile designed to make a woman's heart melt.

"We are," she said, nearly pushing past him toward the door, paper in hand. The man's smile was mesmerizing, and she felt herself falling for him, despite all that had happened with Max. Despite the promise she'd made to herself not to depend on anyone but herself.

"Not until I walk you next door." He reached past her and pulled the door open. She walked into the hallway ahead of him, noticed that Officer Larsen was nowhere to be seen. "Wonder where the security officer went."

"I was wondering the same thing," Sam said, quietly opening the door to Alice's room. "I'll call Nick when I get back to my room."

The room was dark, lit only by the light Alice had left on in the bathroom. But that was enough to show the intensity of Sam's expression. "Make sure you lock up. And you know I'm next door if you need me. Don't go anywhere alone."

"Yes, sir," Kat teased. "See you in the morning."

She closed the door and walked over to the balcony to

double-check the lock. She could see only empty black-
ness beyond. It was late, and she should get some sleep.

But her stomach growled and she didn't feel tired at all.
Johann must have brought the tea some time ago. Her full
teacup sat next to Lillian's empty one on the coffee table,
cold. Too bad it hadn't come with some double-chocolate
brownies. Under normal circumstances, she'd take herself
to the snack bar and then find a piano to play. She'd done
it most nights since taking on this job. The ship had six
pianos, and it wasn't hard to find one in an empty room.

She'd lose herself there for a while. Thirty minutes,
sometimes an hour, until every morsel of tension had fled
her body, and then she'd go back to her room, ready to
sleep. But tonight she'd just have to stay in.

After brushing her teeth, she pulled on her pajamas
and curled up in bed to wait for sleep to come. But she
couldn't seem to close her eyes. She'd left the bathroom
light on—couldn't fathom lying in pitch-dark with all that
had transpired. Surely the security team was scouring the
ship for any other hidden danger. But that didn't give her
much in the way of reassurance.

Who had been in her room?

The same person who had unzipped her garment bag?

She'd almost forgotten about that, would have to tell
Sam and Nick in the morning.

And Morgan...

She closed her eyes, praying for safety, for her friend,
for Jake, for everyone on the ship. Her prayers felt empty.
Silent, cold, unheard.

Still, her heart thrummed with the awareness she'd had
since she was very young. God was there in the silence,
in the empty darkness.

He didn't promise a life without struggle.

She clearly remembered her mother whispering those

words to her one night as Kat had curled up by her in a narrow hospital bed.

But He did promise to never leave you alone.

And He hadn't. Her aunt Malorie and uncle Bob had been there for her for nearly three years after her mother passed away. Then her career had taken off. She'd never lacked for company, was always surrounded by people. Then why did she feel so lonely?

The empty feeling ached, pulsed, overwhelmed her some days. Rising to meet her in the morning and drifting off to sleep with her at night. Taunting her with solitude, empty and dark. Kat had always hated the dark.

Still did.

She turned in bed, restless, but her mind refused to succumb to sleep. She wasn't new to insomnia. Was familiar enough with it to know that no amount of seeking rest would actually bring it.

She sat up, feet curled under her, hair still damp. All was silent, save for Alice's soft snore. It was after eleven, and she should be exhausted, but Kat only felt a tight anxiety twisting in her chest. She glanced over at Sam's grandmother. If only she could be that peaceful right now. Her gaze paused on the nightstand next to Alice's bed.

She'd seen a family picture there earlier and wanted to get a closer look. She padded across the room quietly, bent down to peer at the framed picture. Not enough light in the room. She thought about taking it to the bathroom, curious about the other members of Sam's family. But she felt she was invading Alice's space. Alice's journal sat there also, on top of a black leather Bible.

In her last days, Kat's mother had asked her to read the Psalms a lot. Said the words calmed her and filled her with a peace she couldn't explain. Kat had been surprised to find the words calmed her, as well. She suspected her mother had asked her to read the Psalms as much for Kat's comfort as for her own.

She slipped the Bible from under Alice's journal, held it to her chest and retreated to the pullout couch, propping the cushions up behind her and flicking on her cell-phone flashlight to keep from disturbing Alice.

She pulled the cool sheets up and settled against a couple of pillows, flipping to the beginning of the book of Psalms, skimming and reading, turning the delicate pages and absorbing what she could.

As the minutes ticked by, the words settled over her, bringing a peace and assurance she'd felt once before. She continued to read until her eyelids grew heavy and she felt the unrelenting press of sleep.

But just as her body began to give way to the rest that beckoned, she heard something.

Her eyes flew open.

Rustling.

Something slid against Alice's door, a whisper of movement against solid wood.

Kat sat up straight, straining to hear over the harsh beat of her own heart. Was someone trying to get in? She heard nothing else. Maybe Officer Larsen had come back up. Her hand went to her cell phone. She wouldn't waste time wondering. She dialed Sam.

"Everything okay?" he answered on the first ring.

"I don't know," she whispered, heart in her throat. "I think there's someone outside the door."

EIGHT

"It's just me," Sam said, amusement in his voice. "Sorry to scare you."

"What are you doing out there?" Kat whispered, swinging her feet over the side of the bed. She tiptoed to the cabin door. Pressed her forehead to the cool wood, peered out.

She saw the top of Sam's head, his thick dark hair. From the looks of it, he was sitting in the hallway, back against her door. Guarding the room?

"Nick got back to me a bit ago. Said they didn't find any evidence on the security cameras pointing to an intruder in your room. Larsen was called off from his duty."

"So you're taking over?"

"You planning to keep having a conversation with me through the door?"

A flutter of anticipation coursed through her, but Kat clipped its wings. She'd already talked herself through this. Sam was off-limits. What Kat needed was her life back. Her house rebuilt. Her career back in order. Morgan back on ship.

She didn't need her head in the clouds over a man who was definitely too good to be true. Guarding the room? When would he sleep?

"Right." Her hand found the locks in the dark and she unlatched them, then cracked the door open.

Sam stood there with his phone to his ear and grinned. "That's better." He slipped the phone into a pocket. "I thought you'd be asleep by now."

Kat pushed her hair back behind her ears and kept the door open just a few inches. "I couldn't sleep."

Her stomach growled, making the reason behind her insomnia obvious. Embarrassed, she pressed a hand to her abdomen.

Sam raised an eyebrow, apparently amused. "We never did get those snacks tonight."

She shook her head. "And I left my stash in my room."

Sam rubbed a hand down the back of his neck. "I could use something to eat," he said. "I'm pretty sure the snack bar's still open, if you want to grab a quick bite."

Kat beamed. Sam may be off-limits, but she couldn't refuse his offer, not with these hunger pangs. She stepped out of the room but paused before the door closed.

"Hold on. Let me get my flip-flops."

Sam looked down the hall. "Kat?"

She stopped, her gaze following his, but she saw nothing in the hallway.

"You might also want to get…more clothes," he said.

"Right. I'll just be a minute." Kat slipped back into the room, face on fire.

More clothes, he'd requested. A bubble of laughter threatened as she mentally filed his remark to tell Morgan later.

She quietly grabbed the clothes she'd worn earlier from the chair she'd laid them on, then headed to the bathroom to change. As she closed the door, she caught her reflection in the full-length mirror along the closet door.

How could she have opened the door like this? Her hair

still damp from her shower, wisps of frizz along her hairline, barefoot and wearing skimpy mismatched pajamas.

She changed quickly and ran a brush through her hair. This would have to do. She didn't want the man waiting in the hallway for ages.

Though that was exactly what he'd planned to do. Alone. Doubt crept in as she reached for the doorknob. She should have refused. Should have just asked him to grab her tote from her room. She was just asking for disappointment, spending so much time with him.

Too late to go back now. She opened the door, a little thrill in her step as she walked out into the corridor.

"Let's go grab some food," Sam said.

They walked side by side, arms and hands brushing occasionally as the ship swayed. The corridor was bustling with passengers and crew, surprising for so late at night. Doubtless everyone had been antsy to get out of their rooms, especially the ones with inner cabins and no windows.

"Everyone's just going on as if nothing happened," she said quietly.

Sam nodded. "People see what they want to see."

"Meaning?"

"The captain says it's safe to move around. They all paid a lot for this vacation…they want to enjoy it."

Kat looked over at him. He'd exchanged his black polo for a plain black T-shirt, and it settled just right over his solid chest. She had the absurd urge to scoot closer, slip an arm around his waist and lean into his strength. She forced her attention to the stairs ahead instead. What had gotten into her?

"Or they're just hungry," she said lightly, and Sam chuckled.

"Good point."

"So, were you planning to stay out there all night?"

He nodded. "And it's a good thing. Otherwise, you may have been tempted to take a little walk to the snack bar alone." He looked over at her, and she bristled at his assumption.

"I told you I wouldn't go anywhere alone, and I keep my word." She folded her arms over her chest, defensive. "I also happen to value my life."

He said nothing for a minute as they avoided a line at the elevator and ascended the stairs. Then, finally, "I was just teasing."

Kat nodded, her defensiveness melting. "I should be thanking you. After all, if you hadn't decided to guard the door, I'd still be stuck hungry in your grandmother's room."

Sam laughed softly, and the sound enveloped her with warmth. As far as she could tell, Sam didn't laugh often. She wondered why.

They reached floor fourteen and turned into the snack bar. Ahead, a long line of passengers waited to place their orders. "Looks like half the ship had the same idea."

Sam didn't respond. His gaze steadily searched the room. She could almost hear him cataloging their surroundings, planning escape routes, weighing risks. She half expected him to declare the crowded area unsafe and insist they go back, and she didn't plan to argue. The crowd made her uneasy, too.

"Kat." A voice came from behind them, and Kat bit back the groan that threatened to bubble up. She turned as Max drew closer. He wore khakis and a blue oxford shirt with narrow white striping. His trademark attire. She'd liked it at first—how he always wanted to look put together. Professional, he said. *Just in case I need to suddenly do an interview.* But it had made her feel as though she had to dress the part, too. And, sometimes, she just wanted to lounge around in pajama pants and go to the store wearing sweats.

He stood there with a pasted-on smile, glanced at Sam and back at Kat. "I just got a look at the piano from above. Looks like it was a close call."

"It was."

The line inched forward.

"You two together?" Max asked, attempting a casual interest in the question, but Kat knew better. He was so persistent Kat was beginning to feel a little guilty about her cold response to him. She needed Morgan here to snap her out of it.

Once a cheater, always a cheater, her best friend would say in a singsong voice. But fourteen months together meant Kat had shared a lot of her life with Max. She forgave easily and didn't harbor any bitterness toward him. She simply couldn't trust him and knew he couldn't be depended on.

She wanted to tell him yes, she and Sam were together, anything so he would give up his pursuit. Instead, she looked him in the eye, ignoring his question. "How's your assignment coming?"

"I'm almost done with it already. Just need a few more quotes," he said, confidence spilling out with each word.

"Why don't you go find someone to interview?" Sam suggested, motioning to the crowded room. "Looks like a room full of eager travelers, if you ask me." His meaning was clear. Get lost. And Kat was grateful for it.

He pressed his hand to Kat's back, nudged her forward in line to the waiting cashier.

"Thank you," she whispered, looking back to see Max stalking away.

By the time they had finished placing their order, Max was nowhere to be found, and Kat was relieved. Maybe seeing her with Sam had been what the guy needed.

Sam led them to a quiet booth to share an order of nachos. He waited for her to sit, then slid into the seat across from her.

"So, if security couldn't find anything on the surveillance footage, why did you feel the need to guard your grandmother's room?" Kat asked, snagging a nacho from the basket.

"A lack of evidence doesn't mean there wasn't a crime."

True enough, she supposed, though she wished she could believe everything was fine and go on her merry way. Just like Sam had said, people saw what they wanted to see.

"When would you sleep?"

"I don't need a lot of sleep," he said and sipped his Coke. She believed him. His energy seemed endless. "I'm used to working long hours and night shifts."

Kat snatched another nacho. If she wasn't careful, she'd eat the whole basket of food before he got any.

"Are you having some?"

The corner of his mouth quirked up. "They're all yours."

"We got them to share."

"Only because I knew if I said I didn't want anything, you'd pick something like a pretzel or one of those cold salads."

"And that would be a problem…why?"

"You'd be coming back out an hour from now, hungry again."

"You may be right, but there's no way I can eat all this."

Sam snapped up a nacho. "Now you don't have to."

Kat laughed, but her thoughts circled right back to the lack of evidence from the twelfth floor.

"I wonder how someone could have gotten on my balcony without being seen on the security cameras."

Sam nodded. "Exactly. Unless Security's keeping information from us. They have a lot of freedom since we're in international waters."

"Why would they? Wouldn't it be in their best interest to keep a passenger safe if they found evidence of someone entering my room?"

"Maybe they lost the evidence. Or a surveillance camera malfunctioned. It could be anything, really."

Kat thought about that for a minute, fear taking root at the idea of the security team hiding information at the expense of passenger safety, *her* safety.

"Scary thought."

"I'm just glad you're staying in my grandmother's room for now. Easier to keep an eye out for both of you."

"I didn't want to impose…but I get the feeling she actually wants the company."

Sam smiled, as if she'd just told a good joke. "That's not the only thing she wants."

"What else does she want?" Even as the question popped out, Kat knew the answer. She sipped her iced tea, wishing the words back into her head.

"You and I. Together."

Kat raised an eyebrow, heart thrumming, not sure how to respond. She laughed nervously and ate another nacho, just in case she accidentally blurted out something else. Like *I'm starting to want that, too.*

"She's been trying to hook me up with someone for a while now. Started her scheming about a year after my wife died."

Kat's stomach dropped. He stared down into his glass as he spoke the words, but his pain was tangible, and Kat knew the ache intimately.

"It's been nearly two years." He looked up at her then, stark grief in his eyes. "I think you understand how I feel when I say it doesn't seem to get any easier."

She did understand. She also now understood the edge

he carried around, the emotions he seemed to have such a tight rein on. Loss had changed him, just as it had changed her. She wondered what he'd been like before, if he'd been more carefree with his sense of humor, more generous with his smiles.

She hesitated, didn't want to pry, but also knew from experience that sometimes she wanted to talk about her parents, and most people were afraid to ask. "Can I ask... what happened?"

Sam sat back, and he looked suddenly older, regret tugging at the corners of his eyes. Loss did that, too, Kat knew.

"My job took up a lot of time. I traveled a lot, and I was new, so I didn't have any seniority. I could have made some changes. I was wrapped up in my career."

He stared absently at the half-eaten plate of nachos in the center of the table.

"I was supposed to come home but extended my trip another two days. Volunteered to stay longer to help with an assignment. We'd argued on the phone when I told her. She told me she wanted a husband who would be home to go to the store and get her a pint of ice cream when she was craving it. Not one who thought his career was more important than family.

"She was right. I knew it even when I hung up. I went to my boss and requested permission to go home. Got on the next flight. Planned to surprise her."

Kat's heart pounded a heavy beat against her chest, dread building as she listened.

"But she went out to get that ice cream."

He kept his gaze steady on Kat, wet tears held fast against the memories. "A semi had broken down in her lane. No lights or anything. She slammed right into it. Right about the time my plane was landing."

Kat let out a slow breath, felt tears threatening her own eyes, but words wouldn't come.

"She was pregnant with our first child."

Kat's heart sank. "Oh, Sam…"

He pressed his lips together, and she knew he was holding every emotion in check, just like he'd been trained to do.

"I held her as life support was disconnected," he said "Didn't have a chance to reassure her, to let her know I loved her and that my career would never be first again. We were going to name our daughter Hope. Seems ironic now."

"I'm so sorry," Kat whispered, knowing the words were useless. "It takes a long time to start healing from that kind of loss."

"Not sure you ever do. My family keeps saying I need to let God work on the healing process. The thing is, I'm not ready to let them go. I don't know if I'll ever be ready."

Kat thought about that for a moment, carefully chose her next words. The wrong ones were sometimes more hurtful than no words at all. "I don't think healing always means letting go. Sometimes it means grabbing on—to what you did have, the gift you were given for a while… letting it shape how you live life as you move on."

She did believe that, though she'd been focused more on her losses than her blessings. The house she'd lost in the fire, rather than the ability to rebuild. The ugly scars, rather than her escape from the flames. The sudden loss of her dad, rather than the close relationship they'd begun to rekindle last year.

Sam looked back at her for a moment, a sad smile on his lips. "I needed to hear that tonight," he said.

Then, as if he'd forgotten where they were, he scanned the room again, the wary alertness returning. "We should head back. I want you away from public areas as much as possible. You ready to head up?"

Kat stood. No, she wasn't ready. She would much rather stay in the booth and listen to the low timbre of Sam's voice. She wanted to talk until the sun came up instead of retreating to the quiet darkness in Alice's room. Instead, she scooted out of the booth and walked by Sam's side as he led the way toward the elevator.

Tension crackled between them as they walked. Kat couldn't be sure if it was emotional tension from their conversation or physical tension on her end, but her pulse hadn't let up since she'd seen him sitting outside Alice's door.

They stepped inside the elevator and Sam pressed floor twelve, then suddenly turned to her, the heat in his gaze unmistakable. Her breath caught in her throat. Sam stepped close. He smelled like fall mornings on the lake she and Morgan camped at every October during college... smoldering cedar and morning dew. He brushed a knuckle softly along her lips, and Kat's eyes fluttered closed as the doors began to slide shut.

"Oh, sorry, we can wait—" A woman's voice startled them apart as the elevator doors slid back open.

Sam leaned over and pressed the door-open button. "No need. Come on in."

Three women Kat's age stepped in, all flashing her embarrassed and apologetic looks, and they all rode in awkward silence until the doors opened on deck twelve.

They walked slowly down the hall to Alice's room, and Kat wondered at the near-kiss—how his lips would feel on hers, the tenderness and warmth.

At the door, Sam leaned past her, sliding the keycard, the scent of his cologne faint and alluring. He opened the door for her and she skimmed past him, turning as she entered.

"Are you still planning to sit outside our door all night?"

"Probably." He offered a wry smile, then stepped back. "Get some rest. I'll see you in the morning."

She closed the door and quietly set about changing back into her pajamas. She climbed back into the little pullout bed and closed her eyes. But she knew sleep wouldn't come easily. Not with the lingering heat from Sam's touch on her lips and their conversation fresh in her mind.

NINE

The shrill ring of the phone woke Kat. Darkness shrouded the room, and she reached blindly for the telephone, heart hammering against her chest. She remembered then whose room she was in. The shower was running. Alice must have woken early. Kat pushed herself out of bed and answered the phone.

"Hi, Kat, it's Sam. Did I wake you?"

She blinked, groggy. Glanced at the clock, surprised. It was nearly ten in the morning. "That's okay, I should have woken up a couple hours ago." Her head pulsed with a wretched headache and she moved to grab her purse, rummaging for Motrin.

"I don't blame you. Yesterday was long. Listen, I got the number you were looking for. Do you have something to jot it down with?"

"Wow, that was fast!" Kat set the bottle of Motrin aside and pulled out a pen, taking down the number as Sam read it off to her. "Thank you."

"Sure. Hopefully, your friend is already safely home. Keep me posted."

As soon as she hung up with Sam, Kat grabbed her cell phone to dial Morgan's mother. She saw that she had missed two calls already, both from the Fosters' home number. She must have slept hard last night because the phone hadn't woken her.

She dialed Morgan's mother, holding the phone to her shoulder and twisting the ring on her hand. Praying for good news. By the third ring, she was about to give up and try the cell number Sam had given her, but Lillian finally picked up with a breathless "Hello?"

"Hi, Mrs. Foster. It's Kat."

"Kat!" Lillian exclaimed, and Kat knew from the tone of her voice that the news wouldn't be what she'd hoped. "I'm worried sick about Morgan. Tell me she's okay," Lillian pleaded.

Kat sank into the chair at the desk, dread churning in her stomach. Her friend hadn't made it home. She suddenly wished more than anything that she hadn't made this phone call, that she didn't have to be the one to break it to Lillian that her daughter was missing.

"I was going to say the same thing to you," she said softly. "You haven't heard from her yet?"

"No! I've been trying to get in touch with her for two days. You know this isn't like her."

"When was she due back home?"

"What do you mean?" Anxiety trembled in Lillian's voice, and Kat swallowed back the tightness in her throat. "Why was she coming home?" Lillian asked. "I hadn't heard anything about that. What's going on?"

Kat's mind raced with Lillian's questions, ones she didn't have any answers to.

"I'm so sorry," she began. "I thought you knew she was coming home to be with you and Jake."

Lillian gasped. "Why? Why would she do that?"

"She was worried about Jake... Is he doing okay?"

"I don't understand." Lillian's voice broke, and Kat felt the tears burning her own eyes at the despair filtering through the line. "Jacob is doing fine. He's just fine. Are you sure that's what she told you?"

"I'm sure. So Jake isn't in the hospital?"

"No, he's right here with me in the house. He hasn't been in the hospital for six months." Lillian drew in a quivering breath, and Kat's mind whirled.

Morgan had lied to her.

Why?

They'd shared everything since they were nine years old, had never kept anything from the other. Her mind raced back to the look on Morgan's face that last day.

The fear in her eyes.

It had been out of character, but Kat had chalked it up to Morgan's worry for Jake. She'd always taken care of him, even though she was his baby sister.

Now Kat wondered. If Jake wasn't in the hospital, what had precipitated that look in Morgan's eyes?

"I knew…I knew something was wrong. I just…" Lillian's voice trailed off, and tears dripped down Kat's cheeks as Morgan's mother began to sob. It was a sob that Kat knew too well. The deep, racking sob of loss.

"This isn't like Morgan," Lillian said, voice shaking. "It just isn't." Kat knew it wasn't.

"How did you know something was wrong?"

"She… I—" Lillian hesitated. "I hate to even say it. But ever since she got that raise back in April, she's been wiring me part of the money twice a month. I do okay without it, but it does help with her brother's medical bills and therapies. Nothing came through this time. When I called to check, she didn't answer me. She hasn't called me back…" Her voice trailed off.

"You said she got a raise?" Kat wasn't sure how Morgan could have gotten a raise in April. She'd been promoted back in September, and she hadn't mentioned another raise to Kat.

"Yes, you know, when they made her a sales manager. That's a big pay jump."

"You mean assistant sales manager? She got that promotion last year."

"Yes, but in April they promoted her to sales manager. You know how she's always had such a good work ethic. I told her that would pay off one day…" Lillian broke down again, and Kat felt helpless.

Her best friend had been keeping secrets, and now she was missing.

"What do I do? I don't even know who to call about something like this. Where did you say she got off the ship?"

"Salvador de Bahia, in Brazil. It was our second port of call. July 16. The ship left port at 5:00 p.m. Morgan said she was going straight to the airport to catch a flight home. Maybe you should call the American Embassy in Brazil."

"Yes. I'll do that." Kat could tell that Lillian was barely hanging on to her composure—and her hope. "Thank you for calling me, Kat. I was getting frantic without any word from her. At least now I have something I can do."

"I wish I had better news."

Lillian sniffed. "When I saw messages last night on my phone, I'd hoped it was Morgan…"

"We're going to find her," Kat said. "This is Morgan we're talking about. She's the strongest person I know."

Lillian laughed through her tears. "She is that. Okay, let me try to make some phone calls. I'll call you as soon as I know anything."

Kat disconnected as Alice exited the bathroom, red slacks paired with a cream cashmere sweater, flawless makeup and another wide-brimmed red hat. She took one look at Kat and stopped. "Everything okay?"

Kat sat on the edge of the desk chair. "I just spoke with my friend's mother. Morgan never made it home."

"Oh, no," Alice said. "What do you think could have happened?"

Three light taps sounded at the door. "Let me get that," Alice said and opened the door.

Johann, the cabin steward, stood in the threshold. "I have a delivery from the captain for Ms. Brooks. I was told she has moved to this room temporarily. May I?" He held out a small silver tray, looking past Alice and into the room.

Alice backed up to let the man pass.

Kat watched curiously as he brought the tray toward her, looked for a place to set it down. He couldn't be more than twenty years old, clean shaven with the white-blond longish hair of a surfer. She wondered what had drawn him in; she knew from Morgan and a handful of friends she'd made on the job that cruise-ship employment wasn't as glamorous as it sounded. Fourteen-hour days, cramped quarters and low pay.

"May I?" he asked, gesturing to the nightstand.

Alice picked up her journal and Bible and moved the family picture out of the way. Johann set the tray on the nightstand and smiled at the picture.

"A big family," he said. "Very nice."

Alice beamed. "Thank you, young man. And where are you from? Your accent must make the young girls on this ship swoon."

He laughed. "I am from France," he said. "And my wife would not like the young ladies swooning."

"Must be a hard job to have with a family," Kat said.

He nodded, a wistful look in his eyes. "We have a son." He pointed to a little boy in the photo. Sam had mentioned his sister's little boy. Kat tried to look closer, but Johann moved in front of her to uncover the dish. "Peter is about his age. It is hard. After this contract ends, I will look for work at home. My wife and I, we met on a cruise ship," he said with a grin.

He stepped back to reveal three chocolate-chip cookies and a small plate of fresh-cut fruit. A white envelope rested on the side of the tray.

He paused for a moment, then picked up the envelope and handed it to Kat.

"I will take your response to the captain."

It was a handwritten invitation for tea with the captain at eleven.

"I'll be there," she told Johann. "Thank you."

"Excellent. I will pass on your message."

Alice let Johann out, and Kat took the empty moment to get a good look at the picture. Her focus lit on Sam, and her heart wrenched at the broad smile on his face. He stood behind a pretty woman with straight blond hair and a rounded stomach. Her hands rested below her baby bump, entwined with Sam's.

"My favorite picture," Alice said, sitting next to Kat on the bed. "The last one we have of the entire family."

Kat picked up the frame and looked at Sam's smiling family, their happiness as evident as their bond with one another. She assumed his parents were in the center, right next to Alice and her late husband, and surrounded by Sam's siblings.

"That must be Frank," Kat said, pointing to the man at Alice's side, an arm around her shoulders. He stood tall and proud with not a speck of hair on his head.

"Yes, he was so proud of our big family. And I'm sure you noticed Sam with his wife…"

"He told me what happened. So very sad."

Alice nodded. "Marissa was a lovely girl, and we were all excited about their baby." She looked at Kat. "I keep praying that God will bring another woman into his life. Someone who can bring back that smile."

Sam was right about his grandmother. She really did seem to be pushing to get the two of them together. And after last night…Kat couldn't deny the way her heart thrummed when he was close. But was she capable of bringing back that smile?

Kat looked away, back to the picture where Sam smiled as if everything was right in his world. Her heart broke with the knowledge of what happened soon after.

"Speaking of which." Alice stood, picking up the phone. "I'm going to call over to Sam and let him know you need an escort to the captain's tea."

Kat wouldn't argue. She didn't particularly want to. But she did want to get dressed before he showed up at the door. "While you do that, I'll go ahead and get myself together."

Sam had spent part of the morning on the phone reassuring his mom and dad, who had called in a worried frenzy, and then he'd called his brother to ask for another favor. He was hoping Cody could pull some strings and run background checks on a couple of people. Maxwell Pratt was number one on his list, Officer Tom Larsen a close second. Then, after trying unsuccessfully to get ahold of Nick Callahan for an update, he'd walked several decks of the ship, checking security cameras for any signs of tampering, keeping an eye out for anything that seemed out of place. Anyone who seemed suspicious.

But his thoughts kept circling back to Kat—had been since she'd opened the door last night with flushed cheeks, a bright blue tank top, tiny orange pajama shorts and a head full of still-damp waves.

She'd looked downright kissable.

And he'd almost caved to temptation in the elevator. That would have been a mistake. They were both high on adrenaline and emotion, and he couldn't let his attraction for her cloud his mission: to keep her safe.

At least, that was what he told himself last night, and it would be his mantra today. He'd learned long ago to face one day at a time, and today was no exception.

He walked the length of the hallway and rapped on his grandmother's door. Kat opened it, casting a bright smile up at him.

Despite all she'd been through in life, she still had a determination and hope that couldn't be tamped down. He liked that about her. And it made him all the more determined to protect her.

"You both ready to go?"

"You go on ahead," Alice called from the room. "I have a sudden headache and think I'll lie down for a few minutes."

Kat quirked an eyebrow and Sam winked. "Do you think you'll feel better in time for lunch?" he asked his grandmother from the doorway.

"Oh, I'm sure. You just come get me after you drop off Kat, Sammy."

Kat stepped out into the hallway, looking casual and pretty in dark blue jeans and a gray tank top, long hair secured into a loose ponytail.

"Any updates?" she asked.

He shook his head. "Afraid not." He didn't tell her he'd had his brother run background checks on her ex and Larsen. He'd fill her in if any red flags popped up.

"I've been trying to get ahold of Nick Callahan since seven, but looks like I'm getting the runaround. I keep hoping they've found something on surveillance."

He wasn't banking on that. Cruise ships weren't as secure as they were purported to be, and after meeting with the security team last night, now he understood their limits. Cameras that didn't capture everything, many of which were easily accessible and able to be manipulated due to low ceilings. A small security crew whose only weapons were locked up in the war room and accessible only with the captain's permission. It was the perfect place for the perfect crime.

He glanced at Kat, her profile pale and serious.

"Everything okay?" he asked, and she shook her head.

"I got in touch with Morgan's mom a little bit ago." She looked over at him, fear darkening her eyes. "Morgan's not home…but it's not just that. Morgan told me she was going home to be there for her brother, who was in the hospital. But according to her mother, Jake isn't in the hospital. In fact, Mrs. Foster never even knew Morgan planned to come home."

"But you're sure that's where she was going?" he pressed.

"I'm not sure of anything right now," Kat said, deep brown eyes mixed with hurt and concern for her friend. "But it's what she told me. We tell each other everything. I don't know why she would have lied to me."

"If she didn't tell her mother she was coming, maybe she didn't really plan to go home," Sam suggested. "Maybe she'd planned to do something else, and she didn't want either of you to know what it was."

Kat sighed. "I can't imagine anything she couldn't tell *me*."

Confusion played across her face, and Sam could see that Kat and Morgan had a deep bond. The kind of bond his sisters shared. If the disappearing act wasn't in Morgan's character, then Kat was probably rightly worried.

Sam was worried about something entirely different.

He was worried about Kat and about the timing of her missing friend. Four days after her friend disembarked, the chandelier came down, and Kat had been sure someone had been in her room. Could the incidents all be connected somehow?

"Did she mention anything to you before she left? Give you any reason to believe she wasn't telling the truth about why she was leaving?"

"The only thing that keeps coming back to mind is the look on her face at first. She looked…scared. That was my first thought. But then she told me about her brother, and she was crying, and I just assumed it was the shock of the news." She sighed. "I should have known better," she added. "I should have asked more questions. I'd never seen her like that, and Jake has been in the hospital a lot in the past couple of years."

"You had no way of knowing," he assured her, even though he knew words would never convince her.

"There's something else," she said. "It's not related, but I remembered it last night. Yesterday afternoon, when I was getting ready to perform, I noticed the bag that held my gown was unzipped. All the way."

He waited, not sure about the significance there.

"I know I didn't open the bag," she continued. "And the hem of the dress was dragging the floor. It spooked me because I knew someone had been in my room, looking through my things."

"You didn't mention it to Security yet?"

"I didn't even think about it until last night. Too much had happened."

"We'll make sure we get that to Nick later," Sam said.

"It's probably a good idea," Kat agreed, and he detected a shakiness to her voice that he hadn't heard before. He stopped her on the landing, laid a hand on her shoulder.

"Hey," he said softly. "Nothing's going to happen to you."

Kat moistened her lips, a nervous gesture that unfurled an attraction he hadn't felt for anyone since Marissa. "I hope you're right."

Sam kept walking, and Kat fell into step beside him as

they turned down the hall, a double set of doors straight ahead. "Listen," Sam said. "My grandmother and her friends are going to have lunch in the Emerald Dining Hall. I don't want you going anywhere alone. Go ahead and send me a text when your meeting's over. I'll come get you."

He pulled the door open, and Kat walked past him, her scent reminding him of the honeysuckle he used to pick from his grandmother's garden. Of summer days that he never wanted to end.

Kat waved a quick goodbye, let herself into the dining room and pressed the door shut quietly. When she turned around, Captain Philip Orland was standing so close she almost walked right into his chest. And right next to him, Max. She stepped back, surprised. But, of course, Max would manage to get an interview with the captain for his story.

"Ms. Brooks," the captain said, extending a hand. "A pleasure to meet you. Please, come in."

His white uniform was crisp and tailored to show off his fitness. Barely forty, he had a head full of dark brown hair and piercing sea-blue eyes.

He gently squeezed her hand, the handshake lingering a little too long. She knew from talk on the ship that the captain had a wife and three daughters at home, but she'd heard him flirting with staff on occasion and pegged him as a womanizer.

"Thank you," she said, tugging her hand from his grasp and moving farther into the room.

The captain shifted his attention to Max. "Maxwell Pratt, until this evening." He reached past Max and opened the door for him.

It was a clear dismissal, and Kat read the anger on

Max's face. Still, he hesitated at the door, caught her eye before leaving. "We'll catch up later, Kat."

He left the room before she could remind him that they had no catching up to do. Kat turned to the captain, wondering what had transpired.

The captain looked at her curiously. "You two are acquainted."

"Yes," she answered, though he didn't seem to be asking a question. "I'm guessing he was interviewing you for his article."

"You guessed correctly." He smiled, amusement playing across his features.

"Must have been a hot topic, because he sure left angry."

"He didn't like the answer I kept giving him."

"Meaning?"

"I have no comment at this time." He grinned, and Kat couldn't help but laugh.

"I'm sure that drove him nuts," she said.

"It did," the captain said, looking pleased with himself. "Please." He extended a hand behind him toward a private dining room with several empty tables and enormous windows overlooking endless ocean.

"Thanks for having me." Kat took a seat at the table, set with a pristine white cloth and topped with platinum-trimmed china and a tidy centerpiece of pink roses in a crystal vase.

The captain sat across from her, waiting silently while the server set out an elaborate dessert tray. None of it tempted her. Not with what had happened yesterday and not with Morgan missing.

The captain watched her while the server poured their tea. Unsettled, Kat broke eye contact and set her gaze on the view. Near the helm of the ship, the windows overlooked a sparkling ocean. Nothing to mar the horizon, no skyscrapers, no puffs of pollution. Not even a cloud in the sky today.

"Incredible view," she said to break the stillness in the room.

"Both inside and out," the captain said, attention unswerving from her face.

Kat stared back, uneasy. Was he making a pass at her? "It's a beautiful ship, for sure," she said, hoping that was what he'd meant. "It's a shame what happened to the atrium," she added, wrapping her hands around the warm teacup.

The captain waved the server away.

"Yes, but the atrium can be repaired. I'm just glad you weren't injured. A terrifying ordeal."

"I wouldn't want to relive it."

The captain nodded. "I've heard accounts and seen some security footage. It appears you had a brave rescuer." He took a sip of his tea, expression solemn. "You were very fortunate."

Kat suddenly felt a chill, remembering the events of the previous night and how close she'd come to death once again.

"Sam was in the right place at the right time." She had no doubt God had placed him there for that precise purpose.

"Sam. Yes. The man who saved you. I hear he's a Secret Service agent."

"Yes," she said, wondering how he'd come to that information.

"Last night he offered his help in our investigation," the captain said. "A stand-up man, I'm sure."

Then why did he look so displeased?

"Officer Callahan seems to value his input," he continued. "Of course—" he smiled, even white teeth and shining eyes, and Kat could see suddenly why so many women fell for him "—I'm of the opinion that we have a top-notch security team here on board, and we do just fine on our own."

"Extra hands can only help, though, right?" Kat asked, not sure what the captain was getting at.

"You're absolutely right." He shrugged. "I tend to get a little possessive about my ship and my crew…and Secret Service agent or not, Sam West is just another passenger we need to keep safe."

Kat considered that the ship's security team had so far failed to keep her safe where Sam had succeeded, but she kept the thought to herself.

"So, you *do* think the incident yesterday is cause for concern?"

The captain stared out at the sea for a moment, jaw set in a tense line. "I've been working on cruise ships for almost twenty years." He looked back at her. "Chandeliers don't fall from ceilings."

The hair prickled at the back of her neck.

"That's the reason I asked you here today," he continued. "I wanted to discuss your job. I know you're scheduled to perform this evening in the main theater, but I've decided to cancel the show. And your other concerts as well, just until we have everything settled."

Kat smiled her reassurance. "I have to say, I'm relieved. I'd rather not—"

"However," he cut in, "I am hosting a small dinner tonight. Seems there are many concerned citizens aboard this ship, from all walks of life. Several police officers, a few reporters, Maxwell included. I've had a number of visits and phone calls since early this morning. I'm inviting these passengers to dinner tonight. An intimate gathering that will hopefully settle their concerns and reassure them that we have top-notch security on board."

Kat waited for the part that concerned her.

"I'd appreciate it if you could play some background music. I'll have a piano wheeled in here, and there won't be more than thirty people, I assure you."

When she hesitated, he grinned and pointed to the ceiling. "No chandeliers."

Kat wasn't amused by the joke, but she figured a little dinner music would be safe enough, especially if the guests included police officers and security staff.

"Sure, I can do that."

The captain smiled. "Excellent, excellent. Six-thirty, if you please."

"I'll be here. But, if you don't mind my saying so, I'm surprised we didn't head back to Brazil after the explosion."

The captain nodded. "That's what many of my morning visitors were concerned about. The fire team declared the fire small-scale and contained. And we'd already crossed the halfway point. It wouldn't have been helpful to turn around."

"I see." Kat took another sip of her tea, which was now lukewarm. "Has your team discovered anything new?"

The captain dropped his gaze to his own teacup, and she could see he wasn't about to give her any details. "I'm afraid not." He looked back up at her. "Again, I'm so sorry for what you had to endure. If there's anything I can do for you, I hope you'll let me know."

"Actually, I wanted to mention something to you before we parted ways."

He watched her, curious.

"It's about my roommate, Morgan Foster. She's an assistant retail manager on ship. She left Monday to go back home for a family emergency. Well, that's what she told me...only, I spoke with her mother this morning, and Morgan never made it back home."

Get 2 Books FREE!

Harlequin Reader Service,
a leading publisher of inspirational romance fiction, presents

Love Inspired® SUSPENSE

A series of edge-of-your-seat suspense novels that reinforce important lessons about life, faith and love!

FREE BOOKS!
Get two free books by acclaimed, inspirational authors!

FREE GIFTS!
Get two exciting surprise gifts absolutely free!

2 FREE BOOKS

Love Inspired® SUSPENSE

▲ To get your 2 free books and 2 free gifts, affix this peel-off sticker to the reply card and mail it today!

We'd like to send you two free like the one you are enjoying now. Your two free books have a combined price of over $10, but they are yours to keep absolutely FREE! We'll even send you two wonderful surprise gifts. You can't lose!

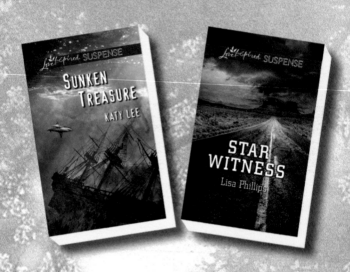

Each of your **FREE** books is filled with riveting inspirational suspense featuring Christian characters facing challenges to their faith.... and their lives!

FREE BONUS GIFTS!

We'll send you two wonderful surprise gifts, worth about $10, absolutely FREE, just for giving Love Inspired® Suspense books a try! Don't miss out—*MAIL THE REPLY CARD TODAY!*

Visit us at
www.ReaderService.com

GET 2 FREE BOOKS!

Love Inspired SUSPENSE

▼ DETACH AND MAIL CARD TODAY! ▼

YES! Please send me the 2 FREE Love Inspired® Suspense books and 2 free gifts for which I qualify. I understand that I am under no obligation to purchase anything further, as explained on the back of this card.

affix
free
books
sticker
here

❏ I prefer the regular-print edition
153/353 IDL GGFW

❏ I prefer the larger-print edition
107/307 IDL GGFW

Please Print

FIRST NAME

LAST NAME

ADDRESS

APT.#   CITY

STATE/PROV.   ZIP/POSTAL CODE

LIS-N14-LA-13

▲ If offer card is missing write to: Harlequin Reader Service, P.O. Box 1867, Buffalo, NY 14240-1867 or visit www.ReaderService.com ▲

BUSINESS REPLY MAIL
FIRST-CLASS MAIL   PERMIT NO. 717   BUFFALO, NY

POSTAGE WILL BE PAID BY ADDRESSEE

HARLEQUIN READER SERVICE
PO BOX 1867
BUFFALO NY 14240-9952

NO POSTAGE
NECESSARY
IF MAILED
IN THE
UNITED STATES

"I'm sorry to hear that," the captain said. "I've met Morgan. Sweet girl. I didn't know she'd left the ship."

"Her mother's really worried, and so am I."

"Is there something I can do?"

The captain looked genuinely confused as to what she wanted from him, and Kat realized she wasn't really sure what she thought he could do. Morgan had left the ship voluntarily, and it wasn't the responsibility of the captain or crew to worry about what happened to her after she exited the *Jade Princess*.

"I don't know. Do you think anyone on board could contact Morgan's mother and walk her through how to go about the search?"

The captain shook his head, regretful. "I'll certainly discuss this with Security, but I don't think there's much we can do in a situation like this. If she left the ship on her own, then where she is now isn't our responsibility. And our hands are kind of full right now…"

"I figured as much. Never hurts to ask. Morgan is—"

A knock sounded, and the door opened. Nick Callahan stepped in, and the look on his face told Kat everything she needed to know. They'd found something.

TEN

"Ms. Brooks, Captain. Pardon the interruption," Nick Callahan said. He directed his focus at the captain. "When your meeting is over, I need to discuss a matter with you."

The captain stood abruptly, clearly reading Nick the same way Kat had. "Looks like our meeting will be cut short."

Kat leaned down to grab her purse and then followed the captain toward the door.

"Thank you for the tea, sir."

"Anytime, and I'll see you this evening."

Nick stood holding the door open for her, and Kat remembered suddenly that she needed to text Sam to let him know she was ready to leave.

"I know you need to get to your meeting, but would you mind if I stayed for a few minutes? Sam was going to meet me here when the meeting was over." The captain hesitated, and Kat added, "He didn't want me walking around alone."

"Are you heading back to your room?" Nick asked.

"Sam's at lunch in the Emerald Dining Hall, and I think I'll grab a bite there, as well."

"I'll take you," Nick said, then addressed the captain. "I'll be back shortly."

"I appreciate your walking me," Kat said softly, keeping pace with his stride. He walked with a slight hitch, but it didn't seem to slow him down.

He glanced her way. "I'm in agreement with Sam," he said. "Don't go anywhere on this ship alone."

"Did you find something?"

He nodded. "I can't discuss it with you yet, but please… be on your guard."

A deep sense of foreboding coursed through her, and Kat stole a glance at the officer's profile. He was just about Sam's height, with blond hair and a strong jaw. His uniform fit to a T and hinted at strong muscles. He had clear blue eyes and a gentle demeanor. But his alertness and energy told her he was worried.

He was tight-lipped as they stepped into the elevator, and Kat suspected she wouldn't get any answers until he'd spoken with the captain. But she'd try.

"I understand that you can't say much, but when you tell me to be on my guard, what can I do? To protect myself, I mean?"

The officer turned steady eyes on her. "Exactly what you're doing. Always travel with an escort. Stay in Ms. West's room if you can. Be alert. Report anything amiss."

The doors slid open, and Nick motioned for Kat to exit ahead of him.

"Do you think someone is—"

"I really can't say any more at the moment, Ms. Brooks," the officer said. "I'm sorry."

She still wanted to press for more, but she sensed the effort would be fruitless. Officer Callahan was tense, his focus fixed on their destination.

"I'm sure when things run smoothly, this is a really interesting job," Kat offered in an attempt at small talk. "Protect thousands of people and see the world while you're at it."

Nick glanced at her, all seriousness. "It sounded just as glamorous when I signed on.

"Here we are," he said. "I hope you can find them."

The man's nerves had rubbed off on Kat, and she was just as anxious to find Sam as Nick clearly was to get back to the captain. She stood at the threshold, scanning the packed seating for signs of Sam and his grandmother. It didn't take long. "I see them."

They were an easy group to locate. Four ladies with ruby-red hats so large that their brims occasionally touched as their heads bobbed in conversation. Kat's lips twitched at the scene—a lone man among four grannies deep in discussion, probably about the events of last night. To his credit, Sam seemed at ease with the group, though Kat took note of his alert posture. This may still be a vacation for most passengers, but for Sam, it had become his job.

His surveillance stopped on her and she waved, heart catching at the easy smile he sent her way. She made her way over to the table, Nick close behind.

"Thanks for the escort," she said to the officer, taking the empty seat next to Sam.

Nick nodded, then directed his attention at Sam.

"I'm sorry I didn't get back to you this morning. I have a meeting with the captain but would like to meet with you and Kat afterward. Can you swing by the office after lunch?"

"Sure," Sam said. "We'll be there."

"Good," said Nick. Then he turned and swiftly left the room, leaving Kat all the more anxious to hear what he was alluding to. She turned to Sam, saw a flash of unease in his expression.

"They found something," he said quietly.

"I tried to press for details on the way down, but he was tight-lipped."

"Kat, dear, I'm so glad you found us," Alice interrupted, the brim of her hat brushing her friend's shoulder.

"The hats are a little hard to miss, Grandma," Sam said, humor shining in his eyes.

Alice's hand came up to adjust her hat. It was simpler than the one from the night before, red silk with an extravagant bow on one side, but the brim was wider than the other and looked a bit unmanageable.

She smiled in agreement. "I suppose you're right, Sammy. Makes your job much easier, though, right?" She winked at Kat and turned to her friends, introducing the three ladies: Ann, Dottie and Norah.

"And this is Kathryn Brooks," Alice continued. "The spectacular pianist I was telling you all about."

"So pleased to meet you, Kathryn," Ann said sweetly, a secretive smile on her lips, and Kat had a hunch Alice had filled her friends in on her matchmaking plan.

"Ann and I went to two of your concerts on ship," Dottie said. "Just lovely music. We could have stayed all night."

"Thank you," Kat said, flattered by the genuine compliment.

Alice sighed dreamily. "I was telling my girlfriends, it sounds like the perfect job for a young woman. What I wouldn't have given to do something like that when I was younger."

"The first two cruises were incredible," Kat said, "but I could do without all that's happened on this one."

After the explosion and some creep following her, and now with Morgan missing, Kat was starting to wish she'd never taken the job in the first place.

"I don't blame you, dear," Alice said. "But just think of all the experiences you get to have, all the memories you're building."

"True enough," Kat said, but her heart didn't agree. She'd traveled a lot during her career, but most trips were rushed and didn't leave a lot of time for sightseeing. Kat had thought that seeing places she'd only read about would breathe new life into her soul. Instead, each new experience reminded her that she had no one to share it with.

It wasn't true, of course. A performance career meant that she was constantly surrounded by people. But her dad had seldom been able to miss work to go with her, and the same went for Morgan. Now her dad was gone and Morgan was missing. Her heart lurched at the thought.

Temporarily, she reminded herself.

Morgan was smart and savvy. She had to be okay. But Kat missed her dad. And her old home. Missed them so deeply that the ache brought to life all the ways she missed her mother. Her dad would have been fascinated by the castles she'd visited in England. Her mom would have loved to take a gondola in Italy.

"How did you get your start, Kat?" Norah asked, and the question brought back a vivid memory that made Kat smile.

"I was invited to perform at Carnegie Hall when I was fifteen," she said. She could still remember the sheer excitement, the pride in her dad's eyes.

"You nervous, kiddo?"

"Nope. I can't wait!"

He laughed. "I'll be nervous for the both of us, then."

She hadn't been nervous at all. Something happened when she sat at a piano, set her hands to the smooth, white keys. She'd never been able to explain it with words, but it was as if she'd been born with music in her soul. She felt the most content when playing the piano, the most in tune with herself.

That was what she'd missed when she was teaching. It wasn't that she didn't enjoy imparting her knowledge to her students, but she missed her hours at the piano, creating, expressing, unrestricted by pedagogy methods and other people's expectations.

"That's where it all began," she continued. "I fell in love with touring and performing, and I didn't want to stop."

She caught Sam's eyes on her, and her throat went dry at the soft look she found there. She sipped her water and was grateful when a waiter appeared.

"Good afternoon," the server said, interrupting their conversation. "Are you joining the table for lunch?"

Most of the group had already finished their meals and moved on to dessert, but she needed to eat something. "Yes," Kat said, turning her attention to the menu, which offered a Southwest Cobb salad, tilapia with rice, or a burger and fries.

"You know you want the burger."

She looked at Sam and caught the teasing glint in his eyes, the barely there dimple on his right cheek. He looked younger when he smiled like that. She wondered how old he was, then reminded herself she shouldn't care.

"You're right. The burger, please."

"They sure *would* make a nice couple, Alice." Norah's whisper wasn't exactly a whisper, and Kat took another sip of water, hoping desperately that Sam hadn't heard the comment. If he had, he didn't let on.

Alice murmured something in a more effective whisper, and Norah dropped the line of questioning, paying extra attention to adjusting her hat.

"Short meeting." Sam finally got a chance to talk as Alice and her friends fell into conversation. "How'd it go?"

"It went well," Kat said. "Tonight's concert is canceled, so that was a relief."

Sam watched her carefully, saw tension drawing her brows together. "I sense more to the story."

"The captain did ask me to play background music for a small dinner tonight in his private dining room."

"You didn't agree—"

"I did. Security will be there. I'm sure it'll be safe enough."

Sam didn't say anything. He knew he had no right to tell Kat what to do, but he didn't think any performances would be a good plan.

She looked at him seriously, uncertainty in her darkening her eyes.

"The captain mentioned you," she said to Sam.

"In what context?"

"I couldn't quite read him. On the one hand, he sang your praises for rescuing me—he saw the video footage. On the other, I got the impression he wasn't sold on your involvement."

"Not surprising," Sam said. "I'm not too worried about what the captain thinks as long as I've got Nick on my side. The captain has the reputation of the ship to worry about. Nick's only concern is safety."

"I hope my food arrives quickly. I'm anxious to hear what Nick has to say." Kat moved to lay her napkin in her lap and her hair slid over her shoulders. He wanted to brush it away, to let his fingers slide over her soft skin.

"I thought I might find you here."

Sam and Kat both turned and found Max standing right behind them. Again. Sam itched to get back to his stateroom and see if his brother had dug up anything on the guy.

"Mind if I pull up a chair?" he said as he grabbed a spare one from a nearby table and scooted to Kat's right.

"I'm thinking we do mind," Sam said and didn't miss the look on Kat's face. Part horrified, part thrilled. From what he gathered from Kat, she was too kind to put the guy in his place. Someone had to do it, and Sam didn't mind stepping in.

Max pretended not to hear Sam, set an open notebook on the table in front of him, jotted down a few notes and looked up. Kat sighed.

"Look, Kat, I know you don't want to talk to me right now. But this is different. I'm not here to talk about you and me. I want to ask you about the explosion in the atrium."

All attention was on him, and Sam could see from the glimmer in Max's eyes that he was soaking it in.

"What about it, Max?"

"You could have died. Can you describe what those moments felt like?"

Kat stared back at him with more restraint than Sam felt. "What kind of a travel piece could you write with that?"

Sam was wondering the same thing.

Max smiled widely, an irritating excitement in his eyes. "I finished everything I could on that one this morning. Until we reach the Islands. I've got another idea I'm working on. Cruise-ship safety. I can probably sell it to a national magazine, especially with what's happened here."

"Good for you," Kat said drily.

"You know how many people go missing off cruises every year?" Max continued. "At least a dozen. Most are never found. Take the explosion in the atrium, for instance. We're in the middle of the Atlantic Ocean, and what kind of security plan is in place if this is the act of some sort of terrorist?"

Ann gasped, and Sam leaned over Kat toward Max, his voice low and firm. "We're trying to have lunch here," he warned. He could understand a journalist's interest in the story, but not Max's egotistical attempt to capitalize on the fiasco.

"Come on, Kat," Max pleaded, not even looking in

Sam's direction. "Just a few words. I need a quote from you, since you were the closest one to the threat."

She shook her head. "Not a good time, Max."

He looked at her for a moment, sighed. "When, then?"

Sam had had enough. He scooted back from his chair and straightened to his full height.

"If she wants to be interviewed, she'll let you know," he said pointedly, moving behind Max so he couldn't be ignored.

Max backed out of his chair abruptly, nearly knocking over Kat's glass of water. She reached out and steadied it, turned wide eyes to the two men as they stared each other down.

Sam actually stared Max down, as Max was a good three inches shorter.

"I don't know what makes you think you can answer for her," Max said, an edge to his voice that grated on Sam.

"And I don't know what makes you think you can keep harassing her," Sam said evenly. "I'm asking you to leave." He glanced at Kat. "You'll call him if you want to talk, right?"

Kat nodded. "I'll call you, Max." And her ex turned on his heel and stalked off.

Sam took his seat next to Kat again, every muscle on edge. The guy made his blood pressure boil. Grandma and her friends had quickly stopped staring and focused their attention on their dessert plates.

Kat looked at him, raised an eyebrow. "You're really riled up."

"You may have dated him for more than a year, but I don't like him."

"I never would have guessed that," Kat said, amusement lighting her eyes. "Thank you," she added.

The waiter served Kat's burger then, and she glanced

at the tiramisu on Sam's plate as she cut her burger into two halves.

"Not going to eat that?"

He shook his head and pushed the plate toward her. "Help yourself."

He was ready to get down to the meeting with Nick and then back to a conversation with his brother. Sitting in the dining room made him feel restless with so many questions needing answers.

He only half listened as his grandmother and her friends hashed out a plan for their afternoon, and it wasn't long before Kat pushed her plate away.

She'd only eaten half the burger, but at least she'd devoured the tiramisu.

"I'm done," she said. "You ready?"

"Grandma?"

Alice sighed, picked up her brownie and wrapped it in a napkin. "I suppose I have to be, since you won't leave me anywhere alone."

She turned to her friends. "We'll catch up later, girls."

"Thanks, Grandma," Sam said. "We'll bring you back up to your room, and then we'll be meeting with Security. We'll come back for you as soon as we're done. I don't think it will be long."

"Really, Sammy," Alice grumbled. "I do *not* need an escort."

He wished she didn't; he didn't want to take any detours. He just wanted to hear what Nick Callahan had to say, no matter what the news might entail.

ELEVEN

By the time Kat and Sam reached the conference room, Kat's nerves were on edge. She was anxious to hear what Nick's team had discovered.

"Right in here," Officer Callahan said, opening the door and letting them pass through. He motioned to one side of the table and took a seat across from them. A laptop was already set up, and Nick waited for them to sit before he spoke.

"What I tell you in this room must be kept confidential," he said. Ice filtered through Kat's veins.

"We've found clear evidence through surveillance footage that someone planted an explosive device on that chandelier."

Nick turned the laptop toward them, scrolling the mouse over and opening a file. "This is what we've got."

Kat leaned forward, and so did Sam, his arm pressing against hers as the footage rolled. The camera angle captured a short length of hallway and part of a balcony overhanging the atrium. The time stamp ran on the lower left of the screen. A little after one o'clock, the morning of the explosion.

"There's your man. Watch carefully. See if you recognize anything about him at all."

He slowly entered the frame, head down and face hidden by a plain black baseball cap. Kat leaned in closer, searching for anything identifying. He wore dark cargos and a black windbreaker. The footage was grainy. She couldn't see if he wore a wedding band on his hand. His shoes weren't visible in the frame.

"And here he goes."

The perpetrator turned his back to the camera and smoothly withdrew a small object from his side pocket. Keeping his hands concealed under the balcony railing, he moved a few inches to his right, stepping just outside of the frame. Only the side of one leg remained visible.

Frustrated, Kat leaned closer to the screen, willing the image to clear up. "Do other cameras capture better angles?"

"Look, right there."

The perp's right hand came into view as he discreetly unfolded what appeared to be a narrow extension pole, locking it one segment at a time, one-handed, as he let the pole extend down and out of the frame.

It was only a matter of seconds. The man was quick. Had likely practiced the maneuver many times before the operation. The pole moved up higher in the frame and couldn't be seen again.

"He used that to lower the device onto the chandelier," Nick said.

The entire clip lasted two minutes and twelve seconds. Then the man casually walked out of the frame again.

The blank screen stared back at them, the time stamp ticking away. Kat watched it, stunned.

A bomb, then.

Had it been meant for her?

"The guy I saw right before the explosion was wearing a dark ball cap," Sam pointed out. "And the person Kat saw in the hallway last night."

"Anything else familiar?" Nick asked.

"Hard to tell. Where'd he come from?" Sam demanded. "There has to be more footage."

Nick looked just as frustrated. "We're looking, Sam. It's as if the guy appeared out of nowhere. We're checking every camera angle for the thirty minutes prior to his showing up at this location. It'll take time." He sent a regretful look toward Kat.

"Whoever's responsible has studied the security system," Nick continued. "He evades the cameras, shows up in different locations and we can't piece together how he got there. We have a couple views catching his arm and the edge of his hat, but nothing to work with yet."

He directed his attention toward Kat. "I have every man we can spare reviewing footage, but I won't candy coat it for you. Our team is large for a cruise ship, but we only have twelve officers, myself included. We're in defense mode right now, because we don't know what we're dealing with."

"Do you have any leads?" Sam asked.

"A few, based on other video footage and times related to the planting of the bomb and also the incident with the lights on deck twelve." He looked back at Kat. "I brought you down here today to see if you recognized the man in the video."

"There's not much to see that would identify him over anyone else," Kat said.

"Anything that you recall from the past couple of days that you haven't reported? Anything out of the ordinary or suspicious?"

"There is something I remembered," she started. "Before my performance in the atrium, I noticed the garment bag holding my gown was unzipped. I hadn't touched it, so I knew someone had been going through my things."

"But you didn't report it?" he asked, jotting down notes as he spoke.

"It didn't seem important at the time. Nothing else had been moved, nothing taken. Then the chandelier fell, and it just slipped my mind."

A warm hand settled over hers on the table. "You're shaking," Sam said.

"I've been convincing myself it was all just a terrible accident. Knowing it was a bomb…what do you think about the timing? And the location?"

"There are really only two possibilities," Sam said. "Either the perp hoped to do more damage, or you were the intended target."

"I agree," Nick said. "We don't know who we're dealing with. A terrorist? A thrill-seeker? Or someone who's targeting Kat specifically?" He closed the laptop.

"We've called in for help," he continued. "But it will be a long time coming."

"How long?" Kat asked.

"Twenty-two hours." Nick's face was grim. "The Spanish Navy is sending a ship."

"She needs a posted guard," Sam said.

"I'm briefing my team in one hour, and I'll put two of my men on a rotating shift. The captain has agreed to unlock the weapons, so we'll be more prepared and effective. Until then, Kat, I suggest you stay with Ms. West and keep to the room as much as possible." He stood, tucking the laptop under his arm. "I need to prepare for the briefing." He opened the door, and Kat and Sam followed him.

"Thanks for keeping us in the loop," Sam said as Nick walked with them into the hall.

"You'll be safer knowing what you're up against, but please keep everything we've spoken about confidential." Nick looked apologetic but firm. "I should warn you, Sam, I've been advised by the captain not to allow you to participate in the investigation. He's protective of his ship."

"But you allowed me into the room," Sam pointed out.

Nick grinned. "You're Kat's friend, right? She needed moral support. Plus, you're a witness to the accident. I'll need to keep in contact with you."

"I appreciate it," Sam said. "We'll head right up to my grandmother's room."

Kat didn't argue, didn't even want to, even though she'd considered moving back into her cabin tonight. The nights had been hard enough since the fire. Alone in her cabin, knowing a bomber may be on the loose, she would never sleep.

Kat leaned against the mirrored wall in the elevator and looked up at Sam, eyes pooling with fear. "Twenty-two hours until help arrives," she said. "That doesn't sound good."

No, it didn't. And he'd give just about anything to get his hands on one of the weapons the captain would be unlocking today. Just in case.

"They don't have enough manpower on this ship," Sam ground out. He looked straight at Kat. "This guy wants to kill. And next time, he might succeed."

"You sure know how to make a girl feel at ease," she said.

"You shouldn't feel at ease, Kat. And you shouldn't leave my grandmother's room until we dock, unless it's absolutely necessary."

Even as the words flew out, he sensed his own desperation and despised it. He clamped his mouth shut and raked a hand through his hair.

How many times would he have to repeat this lesson in life? He wanted to be able to control the situation, the outcome, but he knew he wasn't in control. He never had been. Not when he was a toddler in the home of a drug-addicted and neglectful mother. Not when he was an elementary-school kid shuffled back and forth between foster homes.

Not as an adult when Marissa and the baby had died. And not here on this cruise ship, either.

God was in control, as He'd always been. Sam needed to trust that, but the lingering bitterness of loss made trust nearly impossible.

"Sorry," he said as the elevator descended. "I'm just on edge."

"It's okay," Kat said quietly. "We all are."

They were silent until the doors opened on deck twelve, and they slowly walked toward Alice's room.

"I think you should tell the captain you're not up to performing tonight. He'll understand, in light of the situation."

"I can't do that. I—"

He stopped right outside his grandmother's door. "Look, Kat, as long as you can be out of the mix, stay out of it."

Kat stared back at him, looking somewhat mutinous. She didn't strike him as a woman who took orders from anyone. Sam knew he sounded demanding, but he wouldn't back down. She needed to accept that she was in danger.

"I know you're right," she said reluctantly.

"Good."

"But," she continued, "with Security present at the dinner tonight, I'd like to keep my commitment."

A glimmer of independence shone in her eyes. She was no delicate flower in need of tending, rather someone who knew her mind and wouldn't be slow about using it. He admired that, but it could get her into trouble if she wasn't careful.

"If you can't be convinced, I'll at least escort you there and back."

"I don't expect you to be my personal bodyguard."

"I don't think I offered those services," he said, but for all intents and purposes, that was exactly what he planned to be for her until she was safely back home—her personal bodyguard. He would watch out for her, deliver her back home to Miami, and they would go their separate ways. And she would be alive.

"What I mean is, you don't need to feel obligated to look out for me. Nick said I'd have a guard."

Sam straightened, tapped on the door as he slid his keycard. "There was a reason I was in that room with you when the explosion happened, and unless you tell me to take a hike, I plan to ensure your safety until this lunatic is caught." He hoped she wouldn't tell him to take a hike. He was banking on it. It would be easier to keep her safe if she cooperated, but he would do whatever it took to protect her—with or without her consent.

They still had two full days left until they reached shore. He prayed they wouldn't encounter more trouble before then, but he had a bad feeling they would.

"You two look mighty grim," Alice said as she stepped in from the balcony. "Perhaps I'd better sit down for this." She marched over to her bed and propped up her pillows to get comfortable. He half expected her to ask if she could dial her friends and put them on speakerphone.

"They did make a new discovery in the investigation," Sam said carefully. "But Nick asked us not to share the information with anyone."

"Oh, come now, Sammy. I'm not anyone. I'm your *grandmother*."

"The important thing is that help should be here by this time tomorrow."

"What kind of help?" Alice asked, eyes narrowing as if she could read his mind. He used to be sure she could.

"The Spanish Navy," he said. "But don't go telling your friends, Grandma. If you leak it and Nick finds out, he'll cut me out of the loop."

"My lips are sealed," she said firmly, and he believed her. Grandma was a smart lady and would use discretion.

He still didn't want to tell her every detail. Didn't want to break Nick's trust and miss out on vital pieces of information.

"So, that's all you can give me?" Alice pressed.

"So far, yes."

His grandmother sighed, picking up the book she'd set down next to her. "Then I suppose I'll just sit here and read my book for a bit. This stateroom is beginning to feel a little bit like a jail cell."

"You're being dramatic again, Grandma," Sam said lightly. "Go read on the balcony. It's nothing like a jail cell. Nick's setting Kat up with a guard within the hour," he added. "Once I know she's looked after, I'll take you wherever you and your friends want to go."

He didn't like the idea, but he knew he'd never be able to keep his grandmother in her room. If he refused to escort her, she'd sneak out when he left, and he'd rather make sure she was accounted for.

"Your own guard," Alice said. "I'm even more curious now. But I won't pry," she added. "And, thanks, Sammy. My friends and I wanted to do a round of bowling before dinner."

He barely heard her because his cell phone vibrated, a text popping up. It was his brother.

Sent you an email.

"Okay, let me go back to my room for a minute. I need to check on something," he said, heading toward the door. He was anxious to get his hands on the information Cody had sent. He had a feeling he knew who the information would point to.

His suspicions kept homing in on one person.

Max.

Sam couldn't help but wonder what Kat had seen in

him. What kind of a man followed his ex on board a cruise ship to win her back after three unsuccessful months of trying to win her over? And the guy had cheated in the first place. It wasn't as if he was some doting, committed, love-struck sap.

Minutes later, Sam discovered he'd been right about Kat's ex-boyfriend; the sleaze had a record to prove it.

Sam stalked back to his grandmother's room and opened the door without bothering to knock. Grandma and Kat looked up from their seats, startled.

"Were you aware that seven years ago, Max had a restraining order filed against him?" Sam asked.

Kat looked at him sharply. "What? No, I didn't know that."

"This morning I asked Cody to run a check on Max. And Larsen."

"Did he give you any details about the restraining order?" she asked, grabbing a bottle of water from the fridge.

"Sounds a lot like what's going on with you. He had a girlfriend he wouldn't leave alone after a breakup."

"That would have been when Max was nineteen or twenty," Kat pointed out. "A long time ago. What about Officer Larsen?"

He wasn't sure why she was so eager to defend Max. He hoped it wasn't because she still had feelings for the guy. She deserved better. "Larsen's record is clean."

Kat stood by the balcony door, looking out onto the clear blue horizon. She turned back to Sam, dark eyes serious. "I wouldn't mind seeing that report for myself."

"Let's go, then," he said. "Grandma, we're going to—"

"Go, go," Alice said, grabbing a book from her nightstand. "I'm at the part where the hero saves the heroine and they're about to find their happily-ever-after."

Kat giggled and followed Sam to the door. "I may have

to read that book after you're done with it," she said. But Sam didn't miss the sly grin on Grandma's face, and he suspected his grandmother hadn't reached that part in her book yet at all. Shameless matchmaker that she was.

He entered his room ahead of Kat, holding the door for her. "Have a seat," he said as he pulled the file up again on his laptop. Kat sat next to him on the couch and they leaned forward at the same time, skimming through the information.

"You're right. He was nineteen," Sam said. Not that age had much to do with it.

"He wasn't violent," Kat pointed out.

True enough. But abnormal behavior, nonetheless.

"Plus, her parents filed the restraining order," she added.

Looked as if his girlfriend had still been living at home, and the parents were alarmed by Max's persistence. Good intuition, in Sam's opinion.

"I'd like to ask him about the incident personally," Sam said.

Kat hesitated.

"You don't need to go," he told her, logging out of his email and shutting down the computer. "But he may be more open to talking if you're there."

"I think I'd better," she agreed.

They walked down the hall to Max's room, and Sam knocked, stealing a glance at Kat at his side. Her expression was unreadable.

Sam knocked a second time, but Max didn't answer.

"Looks like he's not there," Kat said, relief softening her expression.

"You have his cell-phone number," he pointed out.

When Max picked up, Kat almost groaned. He'd always been cheap, and she'd halfway hoped he'd have his phone turned off to save on roaming charges. She didn't want to face him, certainly didn't want to be a part of the line of questioning Sam wanted to pursue. But Sam's instinct was spot-on; Max wouldn't answer any of Sam's questions without her there.

"I was hoping you'd call," Max said. "I've kept my cell phone roaming for days."

She had to agree the attention was a little creepy.

"I'm with Sam West," Kat said. "We wanted to meet with you about something."

"I'll meet with you, but I'm not meeting with Sam."

Kat gritted her teeth.

"Let's make a deal," she suggested. "You meet with Sam and me, and I'll answer the questions for your story."

Sam shook his head in an attempt to get her to reconsider, but she knew Max well. She'd only get what she wanted if he got what he wanted.

Max laughed, and the sound grated on Kat's nerves. "It's not like you to play hardball, Kat," he said. "It's a little bit endearing."

She ignored his comment. "Do you agree?"

"Only if I get to ask my questions first."

"No," she said. "You know I'll hold up my end. You're the one who has trouble keeping promises."

"Touché," he said softly. "You win."

She didn't feel victorious in the least. She was in the middle of the ocean with no land in sight, her best friend was missing, a maniacal bomber was on the loose and the cavalry was a long way out. No, she didn't feel victorious, and she wouldn't—not until she got ahold of Morgan and set her feet on dry land.

TWELVE

Max was already waiting for them in a booth when they arrived, a notebook open in front of him, pen in hand.

"I ordered your iced tea," he said. "Two lemons." He smiled knowingly, as if his good memory would convince her to take him back.

"Thanks," Kat said, sliding into the booth after Sam.

Max opened his mouth to say something, but Sam jumped in.

"I'll cut right to the chase, Max," he said, and Max's eyes narrowed, lips pressing shut. "I don't think it's a co-incidence that you got an assignment that put you here with Kat."

"What's your question?" Max leveled his stare on Sam.

"For starters, how'd you really get this job?"

Max blinked, and his expression reminded her of the day he'd come to visit at the hospital and she'd confronted him about his affair. Caught.

"What's it to you?"

"You said you'd answer our questions," Kat reminded him. "Until you do, I won't answer yours."

Max shrugged, an easy smile playing across his lips. "You caught me. I asked for it." He winked at Kat, and she restrained herself from rolling her eyes. "Doesn't that give me brownie points or something? You know travel writing isn't my thing, and I don't have a lot of spare time to go on a cruise."

"I'd say the only thing it gives you is the creep factor," Sam said. "But then, this is nothing new for you."

Max frowned, tapping a finger on the table. "Meaning?"

"Tell us about your restraining order."

Max's eyes widened with disbelief. "Where'd you get that information?"

"I have resources," Sam said.

"Overprotective parents," Max said. "My girlfriend's family didn't like me."

"You mean, your *ex*-girlfriend's parents?" Sam said. "Because according to the file I have, you and your girlfriend had broken up, and the family got fed up with your hanging around, so they filed a restraining order against you."

"That was years ago," Max said, his tone clipped and neutral.

"And here you are doing the same thing again," Sam said.

Max looked down at the blank page in front of him, and Kat felt a tug of pity for him.

"Is that a question?" he asked.

"No, a statement of fact," Sam said.

"My turn," said Max.

"We're not done yet," Sam reminded him, but Max shrugged.

"New rules. I answered two questions, now Kat answers one."

"Go for it, Max," Kat said, because she knew from the look on his face no amount of arguing would change his mind.

"Can you describe what those moments in the atrium felt like—when you saw the chandelier falling?"

They had felt like death. And terror. And the end. "It was terrifying," she said. "Sam, your turn."

"Oh, come on," Max argued. "You have to give me a better quote to work with."

"Why weren't you at Kat's performance in the atrium?" Sam asked, ignoring Max.

"I got caught up in a conversation at dinner," Max said, pen poised for his next question. "How did you get out in time?" he asked Kat.

"I almost didn't," she said. "I jumped up from the bench to run, and my heel got stuck in the hem of my gown... Sam got ahold of me and pulled me away just as the chandelier crashed down. Samuel West," she added. There, now Max had a good quote, and Sam would get some recognition.

"What's the name and number of your editor?" Sam asked, pulling out his cell phone to input the information.

"I don't need to give you that," Max said, and his expression reminded Kat of Morgan's ancient cat, Dumpling, with his scrunched-up face that always seemed put out.

Her cell phone rang, and Kat dug it out of her purse.

Lillian. Kat was almost too afraid to answer. But she did, and the sound on the other end of the line made her wish she hadn't.

She stood from the table, leaving Max and Sam and retreating to a far corner of the room for privacy. She sat on a bench, a hard knot aching in her throat as she listened to the heartbroken sobs coming from Morgan's mother.

"The police..." Lillian started. "They found Morgan's cell phone in Brazil, at the port where she left the ship. It's cracked, like it had been dropped."

"Okay," Kat said, clinging to a shred of hope. "And Morgan?"

"No sign of her."

"It's possible that—"

"Why would she just leave her cell phone if she dropped it, Kat?"

She wouldn't.

"Maybe she didn't realize she'd dropped it. By the time she did, she couldn't find it. Where was it?"

"On the edge of a side street a few blocks from port. I was told it wasn't a street tourists normally frequent. They're doing a search. It doesn't sound good, Kat. If she's…alive…she'd find a way to call."

"We can't talk that way," Kat said. "Morgan is alive. She has to be." Tears streamed down her cheeks as Sam approached and took a seat next to her on the bench. A warm arm slid around her back, tugging her close. She leaned her head into the safety of his chest. Absorbed the offered comfort. Closed her eyes against all the things that could have happened to Morgan.

"You're right. We have to keep believing that. And praying." Lillian could barely get her words out between sobs.

Kat felt ill. It had been only a few days ago when she and Morgan had stayed up late, brought dessert trays into their room and traded hopes and dreams.

"Oh, dear. A friend is at the door," Lillian said. "I'll call you if I hear anything else."

"Okay, Mrs. Foster. Take care of yourself, and remember how strong you raised Morgan to be. She's a fighter."

Kat disconnected and felt leaden, every muscle limp, defeated.

"Not good news?" Sam asked, his hand caressing her side.

"Morgan hasn't been found. But her cell phone was located, cracked, on a side street."

She swiped at the tears that streamed hot down her cheeks, but they kept falling anyway, and Kat leaned into Sam's side. He stroked her back gently, and she gained comfort from the touch, sending up a silent pleading prayer that God would protect Morgan from whatever trouble she was in. Because her gut told her Morgan was alive, but she didn't know for how long.

"You okay?" Sam said after a few moments.

She sat up. "I will be." She took a breath, stood. "They only found her phone," she added. "I have to believe she's okay."

Sam handed her a napkin, and she blotted her tears as they headed toward the exit. "Where did Max go?"

"Off to pout," Sam said mildly. "He tried to follow me over here, but I told him I could easily help you file a restraining order if he didn't start backing off."

"Thank you." She looked at her watch, angst pitting in her stomach. "Pretty soon, I'll need to start getting ready." The last thing she wanted to do was play the piano for a dinner party tonight.

"When are you heading down?"

"The dinner's at six-thirty, but I'll want to find a place to warm up beforehand, around five forty-five."

"I'll swing by at quarter after and walk you."

"Really, Sam, that's not—"

"Humor me," he said, a soft smile on his lips.

"Okay, then. I'll wait for you."

The gown Kat had planned to wear to the concert that night seemed too fancy for the captain's dinner, and her mood didn't match the bright purple hue. So before heading to Alice's room, she'd asked Sam to detour to her own cabin to grab another. It was one of her staples, a black silk sheath dress that skimmed her figure, hemmed just below the knee. Now, standing in Alice's room in front of the dresser mirror, Kat clasped on a new amethyst bracelet to add a splash of color before passing the flat iron through her hair a few more times.

She was about to touch up her lipstick when Sam knocked. Right on time. Kat opened the door and stepped into the hallway, chiding herself for the fluttery feeling in the pit of her stomach and what was shaping up to be a serious crush.

Once they got off this ship, *if* they got off this ship, they would go their separate ways. Kat had been hit with her share of loss in the past several months, and she didn't need to open herself up to more. Still, the lure of companionship teased at the edge of her heart.

Not for the first time, she wished Morgan were here. They'd spent most of the past several years apart, but she'd always been a solid sounding board.

"I'm all set," Kat said, shutting the door behind her.

Sam reached out and slid a tendril of her hair through his fingers, the streak of white peeking out. "Beautiful," he said.

Kat's gaze flickered to Officer Larsen, who had stationed himself a few yards away and was watching their every move. "It's hereditary," she offered. "My mom had it, too."

Something about Sam's proximity, the way he watched her, the way he moved, kept her from forming intelligent thoughts at the moment.

"Interesting, but I didn't mean your hair."

His gaze dropped to her lips, and she wet them without thinking, then blushed crimson.

His hand dropped to his side, and disappointment unfurled in Kat's heart. She could still feel the brush of his knuckles skimming her lips the other night in the elevator.

"Where to?" he asked.

"There's a ballroom on deck seven," she said, reining in her heart rate as they headed toward the elevators. "The schedule's clear, and there's a piano."

"Lead the way," Sam said, and Larsen followed. His

presence was both a comfort and a distraction. A comfort because he was now armed, and Kat knew that he and Sam could take care of any threat that came her way.

A distraction because his cold expression bothered her. He always seemed put out with his job. But maybe he was just intense about it. She tried to ignore his presence as they started down the stairs.

"So, do you get nervous before performances?" Sam asked.

"Sometimes," Kat said. "Depends on the stakes—and the audience."

"Tonight?"

"Nervous…no."

Sam cast a curious look at her. "But?"

Kat didn't know exactly how to describe her feelings about the evening. "My heart's not in it, not with Morgan missing…and everything else going on. I just want to get it over with. Here, to the right," she directed.

"I don't blame you," Sam said as they approached the ballroom. "You can always back out," he reminded her.

"I know you're right, but I feel obligated. I want to follow through."

Sam reached past her and opened the door, letting Kat enter, then looked back at Officer Larsen. "You coming?"

"I'll wait outside," Larsen said.

Kat walked across the room toward the baby grand, heels echoing on black marble. Sam pulled a chair from a stack near the wall and sat down. "Do you mind the audience?" he asked, and the softness in his eyes made her pulse race.

"Not at all," she said, seating herself on the bench and setting her mind to her program. She'd planned a classical concert for that evening, but it didn't fit the occasion, so she decided to bring back the music she had intended to perform in the atrium.

She was more aware of her audience of one than she'd ever been aware of even a thousand people watching. She set her hands to the cool keys and let the music do what it did best—heal, comfort, reach into her soul. One song, then another, Kat let herself get caught up in the melodies, unaware of time or place.

A touch at Kat's shoulder made her startle. "The dinner starts in five minutes."

Kat turned and found Sam had moved close.

"I didn't realize…" She stood, suddenly more aware of the emptiness of the room, the knowledge that it was just the two of them speeding up the beat of her heart.

Sam reached for her hand and slipped her arm into his, leading her toward the doors. "I could listen to your music all night," he said. "I don't know how you do that…weaving stories with no words."

"Thank you," Kat said, and she knew he wasn't just flattering her. Could see truth in his eyes. In just twenty-four hours, Sam had an understanding of her that Max had never been able to glean in the fourteen months they'd been together.

Officer Larsen was leaning against the wall as they came out, his trademark scowl firmly in place, and he followed behind as Sam and Kat made their way back up to the captain's dining hall.

At the door, Sam paused, looked at Larsen. "Will you be attending?"

"Yes, I'll be there for the duration," Larsen said with a resigned tone.

"My grandmother wants to go bowling," Sam said, turning back to Kat with a similar resigned tone. Then he leaned close to her ear, his soft whisper rolling down her spine. "Give me a call when the dinner's over," he said. "I'd like to walk you back, even though Larsen's here."

She nodded, stepping out of the lure of his closeness. "I

will," she said, moving into the room and away from the only person on board who made her feel safe.

Several people already milled around the room making small talk. True to his word, Captain Orland had gotten a piano wheeled in. A silver baby grand. The captain caught her eye and walked over to her. "Welcome, Ms. Brooks," he said. "Have something to eat before we get started." He pointed over to the buffet.

"Thank you." She headed to the buffet, but the roast beef and potatoes just looked heavy and turned her stomach. She grabbed a roll and put it on her plate, adding some cheese to the side, and turned to find Nick Callahan next to her.

"I spoke with Sam earlier," he said. "He told me about Morgan Foster. I hope your friend is found soon and that she's okay." He had kind eyes, and she wanted to tell him to stop looking at her that way, because she didn't want to break down right there at the dinner.

"Thank you," she said instead. "I appreciate it."

"I've put in a call to the police department in Salvador de Bahia," he added. "Asked that they keep us informed about the case. I'll pass on to you anything I'm at liberty to share."

"That means a lot, thank you."

"They've also asked me to pass on any new information to them. So, if you think of anything that might help, come talk to me."

"I'm not sure what I have to add, but one thing has been bothering me," Kat said reluctantly. Now was as good a time as any, and she'd only help her friend by being forthright. "Morgan's mother told me that Morgan has been wiring her money every two weeks since April—after Morgan was supposedly promoted from assistant sales manager to sales manager. Only, I'm pretty sure that Morgan didn't get a promotion…"

Nick nodded, understanding dawning. "I see. I'll look into that and pass the information along. And, again, come by if you think of anything else."

"I will," Kat said. "Thanks."

She made her way to the piano as guests piled plates full of food from the buffet and found seats among the six round tables that had been set up in the room.

"Welcome, everyone, to dinner." The captain's voice cut into the din of conversation, and the room hushed. He stood near the wall of windows, white uniform crisp, a welcoming smile on his face. "I've gathered you all here tonight in the hopes of answering questions that have been brought to my attention and reassuring you that my team is working hard to ensure your safety and the safety of all our other guests and crew."

Kat's mind drifted as the captain spouted technical details about their security team and surveillance monitors. Despite all their best efforts, someone had still managed to get an explosive on board and rig an accident that had the potential to cause a lot more damage than it actually did.

She glanced around the room, noted the serious expressions on faces, and her eyes caught on Max as he walked toward her. He winked and she sighed.

He offered her a glass. "Iced tea?"

She wanted to say no, thanks. That she'd started to prefer lemonade, actually. But she was thirsty and accepted the tea anyway. She was relieved when Max simply returned to his seat. She didn't feel like talking to anyone right now, most of all Max. She took a long draw of the tea and tried to focus back in on the captain's words.

Officer Larsen approached and stood in her line of vision. "After dinner, another officer will take my place for the night shift," he said quietly, gesturing for her to follow. "I'll introduce you."

Kat reluctantly set the tea down on the piano bench and

followed the officer across the room to the two security officers flanking the doorway.

"This is Officer Duncan Byrnes," Larsen said, pointing to the man on the right.

Officer Byrnes was over six feet tall and trim. He wore his dark hair cropped close and smiled affably, the polar opposite of Larsen. He extended a hand. "Nice to meet you, Ms. Brooks." She shook the offered hand.

"Will you be returning to your stateroom after the dinner?" Byrnes asked.

"I believe so," Kat said. "And you'll be working the night shift?"

"Yes, eight this evening to eight in the morning," he said.

"Twelve-hour shifts. That's tough," she said, glancing over at Larsen. But he'd already slipped away.

"We're used to it," Officer Byrnes said simply.

"So, thank you for coming tonight," the captain was saying. "I hope you will enjoy the evening."

"I'd better get back," Kat said to Officer Byrnes and moved back to the piano.

"While we eat, I'll take any questions you have," the captain continued. "And I'm confident you will retire to your staterooms tonight feeling reassured that you are all in good hands."

Kat picked up her glass and wiped the condensation off the piano bench before sitting, sipping the tea as the captain wrapped up his speech. Finally, he nodded to her, and she set the empty glass down on the floor, set her fingers to the keyboard and began to play.

An hour of music wasn't difficult for Kat, especially this type. She could play for hours, letting the rush of notes heal her soul. Only tonight, she was suddenly very tired, fighting the heaviness of her eyelids.

The first wrong note startled her. Slips weren't customary for her, and it was her first sign that she'd been distracted lately. But then she hit another, and the keys seemed to blur under her hands, the sound slowing and ringing loudly in her ears.

"Is she okay?" she heard someone say, only the voice seemed to echo from far away, as if Kat were in a tunnel.

She stopped playing, limbs heavy and slow. Something wasn't right. She turned on the bench, tried to stand, but her legs felt leaden, and she couldn't push herself up.

Strong arms gripped hers from behind, helped her up. "You don't look well," Officer Larsen said. "Let me help you back to your room." She felt unsteady on her feet and let him lead her away from the piano, the other dinner guests swimming in her vision. She was dizzy. Nauseous. Willed herself not to throw up in front of her audience.

"Kat!" For once, she welcomed Max's voice. He was at her side in an instant. "I'll help her," he said to the officer. "She's a friend."

"I'm handling it," Larsen said gruffly, and Kat found her footing, leaning against the officer as he helped her out of the room, Max pressing in at her side.

She wanted to tell them that she needed a doctor, not her room. Opened her mouth to say so, but no words would come out.

Something was horribly wrong. Her eyes drifted shut, but she forced them back open, certain that if she gave over to sleep, she may never wake up.

"Finally," Grandma Alice said as they left her room. "I've been cooped up all day." Sam would rather park himself outside the door of the captain's dining hall than sit through two rounds of bowling with Grandma and her friends, but he knew Kat was secure enough where she was, and he couldn't neglect his grandmother, the one person he'd been sent to watch over.

He pulled the door firmly closed behind his grandmother and stopped short at the sight of the entourage coming down the hall.

Kat. Flanked by Officer Larsen and Max Pratt, and Kathryn didn't look well.

Adrenaline surging, Sam jogged down the hall to meet them, more alarmed as he drew closer. Kat's skin was pale, her steps slow and unsteady.

"Kathryn!" Grandma exclaimed, a hand coming out to touch Kat's arm.

Sam looked from Larsen to Max. "What are you doing?" he demanded.

Max glared at him. "We're helping her back to the room. Something at dinner made her really sick."

"She's not doing well," Larsen said. "It hit her quickly. We should have taken her to the infirmary. We'll get her in the room and call the doctor to come up."

Sam leaned close as the two urged Kat toward his grandmother's stateroom.

"Kat." Her eyes slowly turned toward him. Glassy, confused. He bent closer. Said her name again. Still nothing. She didn't move a muscle.

Max was struggling to keep her upright as Grandma swiped her keycard and Larsen pushed the door open.

And then Kat's eyes rolled back and she went slack.

The deadweight was too much for Max, and Sam caught Kat as she slipped from her ex's grip.

THIRTEEN

"Oh, no," Alice said, horror dripping from the words.

For just a moment, fear gripped Sam and his feet froze in place. But he could see the slow rise and fall of Kat's chest. She was breathing.

Sam said her name again, just an inch from her face, urgency building. But he knew she wouldn't answer. Knew it from the slackness of her jaw, her pale complexion in the dim light. He pulled her close, gathered her too-light body into his arms.

"Don't move her!" Max said and then looked at Officer Larsen, who hovered over the group with worry. "Get help!" Larsen pulled out his radio and called down to the infirmary, but Sam wouldn't waste time. He headed toward the elevator, cradling Kat in his arms, Max, Larsen and his grandmother at his heels.

Sam pushed the down arrow on the elevator, impatiently waiting for it to open. He'd memorized the ship's layout, knew exactly where the infirmary was.

A memory assaulted him. Another body, slack in his arms. Long blond hair matted to her scalp, dark with blood. The curve of her stomach swollen with their baby. Sam kicked the elevator doors. Alice's hand came to his arm. But she said nothing.

Sam looked down into Kat's face. She was alive but

unconscious. He had held his wife as her life ebbed away, face paling, breath slowing. Kat's breathing was even, her skin warm. She would be okay. She *had* to be.

The elevator doors slid open and Sam stepped on with his grandmother. Max made a motion to board the elevator behind Larsen, but Sam shook his head. "Stay out or I'll throw you out," he said, anger hot and fierce. Max had no right to be there. Kat's ex retreated, surprisingly, and the doors closed, tense silence thickening as the car descended low into the ship.

When the doors opened again, Larsen stayed behind. "I'll report to Callahan and return shortly," he said, but Sam barely heard him.

He bolted from the elevator and rushed down the hall toward the clinic, holding tightly to Kat. A short man with graying hair opened the door as they neared, his gaze homing in on Kat's form. He opened the door wider, urgently gesturing for Sam to enter.

The doctor motioned to the examination table, concern drawing his eyebrows together.

Sam carefully set Kat down.

The doctor pulled out his stethoscope and began to listen to her chest. "What happened?"

"I'm not sure. She's the pianist for the ship, and she was playing for a small dinner party with the captain. She started feeling sick and was escorted to her room. I saw her condition and brought her here."

The doctor's gaze left Kat and drew back up to Sam. "Her name?"

"Kathryn Brooks," Sam said.

"Age?"

"Twenty-six."

The doctor's eyes narrowed. "And you are related in what way?"

Sam got the impression he was about to be kicked out.

"We're friends."

The doctor looked past him to Alice. "Your relation to the patient?"

"Also a friend," she said.

The doctor nodded. "I'll need you both to wait outside."

Sam was reluctant to go, uneasy leaving Kat in anyone's care, even the doctor's. He watched closely as the doctor gathered some items from a drawer near the sink. A nurse busied herself taking Kat's blood pressure and preparing to draw blood.

The doctor looked up, then pointedly toward the door. "If you please…"

Outside the room, Sam stood next to his grandmother, both leaning against the wall. He closed his eyes and offered up a silent prayer, for safety for Kat, wisdom for the doctor and the ability to protect.

"What do you think?" his grandmother asked. They were the only two in the long hallway, an eerie silence settling around them.

He shook his head. "I couldn't say."

A halfhearted smile tugged at the corner of Alice's mouth. "Looks like now you have to look out for *two* females who seem destined for trouble."

Time passed slowly as Sam waited for the doctor to finish examining Kat. He paced the corridor, tension throbbing at the base of his neck.

"I wonder what happened," his grandmother said for the third time since Kat had been admitted to the infirmary. Sam reined in his patience. To be fair, he hadn't been sleeping well, and he was frustrated with his own limits in the case on the ship. Grandma was just being Grandma, and he didn't want to take his frustration out on her.

"Hopefully, we'll know soon," he said.

All his effort, checking backgrounds, searching the

ship, trying to watch out for Kat at all times, and he still hadn't been there to protect her. Still didn't have enough to go on to keep her safe.

Except instinct.

And instinct told him Kat was in more danger than ever. Whoever was after her had tried several times and failed. The perpetrator was determined, angry and—judging from tonight—getting reckless. And his suspicion about Max's involvement had heightened considerably. He didn't believe for one second that Max had been there by chance. It had been obvious Kat needed medical attention. Why would the guy bring her to her room? Even more questionable, why didn't Officer Larsen clue in to Kat's condition sooner?

The door to the exam room opened. Sam straightened, and Alice followed. The doctor stepped into the hallway, closing the door firmly behind him.

"Kathryn is going to recover just fine," the doctor said. "I'm sure you understand that I can't divulge medical information to you," he continued carefully. "When she wakes, we'll go over the details with her, and of course, it will be up to her what she shares."

"How long until—" Sam started.

"I can't tell you anything further," the doctor said, cutting him off.

"I plan to stay outside this door until she recovers," Sam said, leaving no room for negotiation.

"You're welcome to," the doctor said. "But it could be a while."

Footsteps echoed from down the empty hallway, and Alice and Sam turned to see who approached.

Nick Callahan. He offered a handshake when he arrived. "How is she?" he asked. "Looked like food poisoning or something. Larsen and Maxwell Pratt seemed to have everything under control or I would have gotten involved."

"She passed out when they got her to her cabin."

"That's what Larsen told me."

"It was obvious she needed a doctor," Sam bit out.

"Larsen said he could see it as they got off the elevator. He didn't want to waste any more time."

Sam didn't know what to believe, but he had a feeling that the perpetrator was close, too close.

Pain. Sharp, throbbing, aching pain. Pulsing through her skull with such intensity that Kat couldn't open her eyes. Or simply didn't want to. But someone was saying her name, and she had the urgent feeling that she needed to open her eyes. No matter how painful, no matter how hard.

She squinted, relieved that the light in the room was dim, nearly dark.

"Good girl." Someone whispered the words, and Kat tried to focus on the person hovering over her bed.

"Kathryn, I'm Nurse Sutter. You can call me Abby. You've been unconscious for the past five hours, but you're going to be just fine." Her words came out in a slow, steady stream of calm.

But Kat's pulse was anything but calm. Her heart raced, her gaze darting around the room. Trying to piece things together, pull the memory fragments into a cohesive unit.

"What happened?" Her voice sounded foreign to her own ears, uncertainty and fear crackling along her dry throat.

"Let me call Dr. Henry and let him know you're awake. He'll explain everything to you."

"How did I get here?" The question came out an urgent plea as Kat reached desperately for memories.

The last thing she could remember was the keys on the piano blurring, her hands moving as if in slow motion.

A gentle hand settled on her shoulder. "Try to be calm," the nurse said. "You were very fortunate, and you're going to be just fine. Someone named Samuel West brought you to the clinic a little after seven."

Sam. His face flashed in her mind. Of course. Saving her life once again, presumably.

A door opened, and footsteps shuffled across the room, rubber soles on tile. It hurt to move, so Kat waited until a profile came into view.

"Hello, Kathryn, I'm Dr. Henry." His eyes were kind, his voice gentle and calming. "What is your pain level?"

"Intense." She grimaced at the pounding headache, her mind filled with questions she didn't have the energy to ask.

"We'll bring you some painkillers. It may take another twenty-four hours until you feel completely yourself. In the meantime, you'll continue to experience some of the aftereffects we can't do much about. Light-headedness, the shakes." He stood directly over her, and she tried to keep her eyes open, trained on his face.

"I'm sorry to tell you that you were the victim of a drug known as GHB, or gamma hydroxybutyrate. It's a central-nervous-system depressant, often used as a date-rape drug."

Horror washed over her, but the doctor patted her hand. "Fortunately, it appears that you were brought to us before whoever slipped you the drug could make good on whatever he'd planned."

"But how—" Her voice trailed off as she reached for memories, but nothing was there to retrieve.

"Try not to worry. Your memories will return, and hopefully, you'll recall some details to help Security investigate. Until then, we'd like you to stay here so we can keep an eye on you."

"For how long?" she asked, and her throat was raspy, dry.

"At least for the day," the doctor said. "Rest for a bit. Security will need to ask you some questions. But they'll likely want to question you again later, once your memory fully returns."

"Thank you. Can you let Sam and Alice West know that I'm awake, that I'm okay?"

"Sam has been waiting outside this door since he brought you down here," the doctor said. "We'll bring him in after you've spoken with Security."

He'd been waiting outside the door for her. For five hours. She wanted to hear from him firsthand what had happened. Wanted to see him. Now. Not after Security asked their questions.

"I'd like him to be here," she said as the doctor opened the door.

"What's that?" he asked.

"Sam. I'd like him to be here while I'm questioned. Please."

The doctor hesitated, then nodded. "Of course." He stepped outside, and she heard him say, "She's awake. You may—"

Sam appeared at the door, rumpled hair and wrinkled T-shirt the only signs that he'd been waiting up all night in the corridor outside the infirmary.

He crossed the room, eyes flashing with worry. He brushed her hair back from her forehead, a tender gesture that sparked girlhood dreams of knights in shining armor and happily-ever-afters.

Sam's assessing gaze swept over her, and she could only guess how ragged she must look. Not that it should matter, but it did—there was no sense denying it. She'd glimpsed a true hero when he'd saved her in the atrium, but she hadn't realized how spot-on she'd been. Sam put other people first, risked everything for strangers. There were heroes, and there were superheroes.

Sam's gray T-shirt clung to a muscled chest, and even his five-o'clock shadow and rumpled hair only made him look more attractive. He definitely fell into the superhero category.

Not fair that he kept seeing her at her worst.

"How you feeling?" he asked.

"A little better." She met his eyes, lost herself a little in his gaze. "So you did it again. Saved my life."

He didn't smile, just looked seriously back at her, waiting, she knew, to hear what the doctor had told her.

"The doctor says it was GHB," she said.

He pressed his lips together, cold anger in his expression. "I suspected."

"I don't remember much yet," she told him. "The doctor said it will come back to me…but the last thing I remember is that I was playing the piano, and everything looked blurry."

She swallowed. "My throat is so dry."

Sam looked around. "Here." He walked over to the watercooler and poured her a cup.

Kat pushed herself to a sitting position, holding out a shaking hand to take the drink. "Thank you."

"The shaking is part of the aftereffects?" he asked.

Kat nodded, the cold water soothing her parched throat. "What happened?" she asked. "How did you get to me? You weren't even at the dinner."

Sam took the empty cup from her and tossed it in the trash can. "I was heading out with my grandmother so she and her friends could bowl. I saw you coming down the hall leaning on Max and Larsen."

"Max?"

"According to Nick, Max offered to help you when you started feeling bad. I caught up with you three, and you passed out."

"And you brought me here?"

He nodded, and heat crept up Kat's neck at the image of Sam carrying her through the ship.

"Where's Alice?"

"She's sleeping." He smiled. "She was determined to stay down here with me, but I asked Nick to take her back up to the room."

"And Max?"

"He's tried to check on you three times. I finally asked Nick to keep Max away. Haven't seen him since."

A tap sounded at an adjoining door, and Nurse Sutter walked in. "Sorry for the delay," she said. "I have your pain medicine for you." She handed Kat two small pills and a cup of water.

Kat took the pills and handed the cup back to the nurse. "Thank you."

"You're welcome. Officer Callahan asked to see you. I'll go let him in." She moved to the door and peeked out. "Here he is," she said, opening the door wider.

Nick Callahan walked in the room with the heavy tread of a man heading into a war zone. "It's good to see you awake. How are you feeling?"

"Not great."

"I'm sorry to hear that. And I'm sorry for what you've been through." He pulled up a chair. "I'd like to give you more time to rest, but we don't have that luxury. I need to ask you a few questions, if you feel up to it."

Kat nodded.

"Tell me what you recall about last night."

"I remember the dinner, playing the piano. I just remember feeling dizzy and weak. It was very sudden."

She watched as the officer jotted down notes on a small pad.

"Can you recall any conversations?"

"No, I just have a vague impression of a lot of people around me."

"We spoke at the dinner," he said. "Does that ring a bell?"

Kat thought for a moment, but she couldn't retrieve the memory. "No." She sighed. "I'm sorry."

Sam's hand slid over hers on the cool white sheet and he squeezed gently, reassuring her.

"Don't be," Nick said. "It will come back to you. Let's try to go backward. Did you notice any physical symptoms before leaving your room?"

"No. I felt fine."

"Did you have anything to eat or drink in the hour before leaving your room?"

Kat shook her head. "No. After our meeting, I went back to Alice's room, and then later with Sam to rehearse before the dinner." She glanced at Sam, her gaze dropping to his hand on hers, where his thumb lightly smoothed over the top of her wrist.

His touch was a balm to her frayed nerves, and her eyelids drooped, fighting sleep.

"I can see you're exhausted. I'll let you rest," Officer Callahan said. "Call me as soon as you remember any new details, even small ones."

Sam stood as Nick turned to leave, walking him to the door, and Kat let her eyes shut, the headache dulled and sleep beckoning. But her mind wouldn't rest, dark fear unfurling. Someone on this ship wanted her hurt. Or dead.

Warm fingertips traced over her brow, knuckles brushing gently down the side of her face. Kat opened her eyes and met Sam's tender gaze, felt a tug at her heart that felt nothing like fear and a whole lot like hope.

"I should have told the captain I wouldn't do any more performances on this cruise."

"I should have stayed in that dining room with you."

"You didn't have any reason to, not with Nick and Larsen and the captain in the room." She let out a steadying breath. "I'm scared, Sam," she admitted. And the tears wouldn't hold. She swiped them away, despising her own vulnerability.

Sam stilled her hand with his and sat next to her, tugging her close and slipping an arm around her shoulders. "There's no shame in tears," he whispered, and Kat adjusted her position to lean her head against his chest. She breathed in the faint scent of soap and spice, committed to memory the warmth of his touch.

His fingers brushed the side of her neck, traced the underside of her jaw, and Kat listened to his steady heartbeat. What was it that made him so driven to protect her? She'd felt drawn to him almost immediately, and the feelings were only intensifying. Did he feel it, too? She was afraid to hope.

Perhaps, even, if she were honest with herself, she was afraid to care too deeply. Because the deeper the love, the deeper the ache of loss.

She was old enough to recognize a pattern in her few relationships. Dating men she cared about but didn't feel reckless with. Men she could be just as happy with as she could be without.

Back home, she would have taken one look at Sam and run in the other direction. Just the touch of his hand on hers made her want to forget that loss was inevitable. Made her want to cling tightly to a dream she'd been pushing away for too long—the dream of binding love and a family. But she wasn't the type to cling.

She pushed herself up a little higher, scooting away from Sam's touch.

"We're going to find this guy," he said, letting his arm fall away and moving back to a nearby chair. "We have to."

Before it was too late.

He didn't say it, but they were both thinking it.

"I guess Security hasn't found anything new?"

Sam shook his head. "I've been nosing around the ship myself. The cameras don't catch every angle. It's likely this guy knows his way around."

"Someone on the security team?"

"Possibly. But there are a lot of crew on this ship, a lot of people who know the system."

"Don't they have people manning the footage at all times? How could they not notice anything?"

"Six hundred cameras," Sam said. "That's how many are on this ship. Four members of the security team monitor the footage in shifts, two at a time, 24/7."

"Two people watching footage from six hundred cameras?"

He nodded. "They can see forty angles at a time, so in real time, they see less than ten percent of what's going on here."

"What's the point, then? Are the cameras just for show, just to trick passengers into feeling safe?"

"The footage is, at least, all recorded. But it'll take a lot of time to screen through every hour from every camera. I wouldn't discount someone on Security," Sam agreed. "But Max is at the top of my list of suspects."

Kat shook her head. "It just doesn't make sense. Max isn't dangerous, just annoyingly persistent."

Her sincerity gave Sam pause. She'd dated the guy for more than a year, knew him better than he or any of the security team did. But people like Max often hid a dark side.

"Let's look at the facts, Kat," Sam said. "Max has a history of harassment. He wouldn't leave you alone back in Miami, then he requests a writing assignment that he normally would never work on so that he can follow you onto this cruise ship. He claims he's working on a travel piece, but then latches on to a new idea to write a piece on cruise-ship safety. Meanwhile—"

"Really," Kat cut in. "I think you're—"

"Hold on, hear me out. Meanwhile, Max is inexplicably not present during the one concert when you're nearly killed in an explosion, and he was at the dinner party last night. Not to mention, he was trying to escort you to your room when you obviously needed a doctor."

Kat had paled, and Sam felt like a jerk. She was recovering from being drugged, was clearly scared for her life, and he wouldn't let up. "I'm sorry."

Kat looked back at him, uncertainty in her deep brown eyes. "The iced tea," she said. "Max brought me an iced tea. I remember now..."

FOURTEEN

Security had taken Max in for questioning, and they were searching his room. Having an answer should have settled Kat's nerves, but doubt niggled at the edge of her mind as she retraced the steps she'd taken hours ago. Waking up in Alice's room to the alarm, dressing for the evening. Yes, she could remember that part now.

In her mind's eye, she watched the past evening play out. Sam's eyes flashing when she stepped out of her room, practicing in the ballroom, the walk to the dining hall. Seeing Nick, and Max. Speaking with the captain. Grabbing a roll from the buffet. Drinking the iced tea.

Two lemons.

Max had brought it to her, yes, but did that mean he'd drugged her? Memories swirled in her mind, intertwining with unanswered questions. Kat needed answers. Had Security finished questioning Max? She hoped Sam or Nick would be by to update her soon.

Even though it was barely noon, the room was nearly pitch-black with no windows and just a small desk lamp left on, at her request. The doctor had ordered her to rest, but sleep eluded her. Her worries drifted to Morgan again and she wished she'd asked Sam to bring her cell phone down.

She hoped the doctor would come back soon and release

her. Kat still didn't feel like herself, but she was more than ready to get out of the infirmary.

A knock sounded at the door, and Nurse Sutter walked in from the adjoining room. "You awake, hon?"

"Yes," Kat said. "Would you mind turning on the lights? I can't sleep anyway."

"Of course." The nurse flipped on the overhead lights, stopping near the entrance to the infirmary. "Officer Callahan is outside and would like to speak with you, if you're up to it."

"That would be fine," she said, and the nurse opened the door to let the officer in. Nick stepped into the room, Sam right at his heels. They wore nearly identical expressions, faces serious and full of news Kat wasn't sure she wanted to hear.

"What's the verdict?" she asked.

"I have mixed news," Nick said. "The navy ship has been delayed, won't get here until later tonight. But it's possible we don't need the extra hands." He paused, then came out with it. "We've detained Max in the brig," he said, and Kat's heart dropped. "While we questioned him earlier, I had two of my men search his room. They discovered a small vial of clear liquid. Dr. Henry tested it and confirmed it to be GHB."

Kat couldn't dispute the facts, but she also couldn't quite believe them. How could she have dated Max for so long and known him so little? Had he really wanted to harm her? Or did he have some sort of sick idea of how to make his article more interesting? Neither idea resonated with what she knew of Max. He'd never struck her as a dangerous person. Selfish, yes. Arrogant, yes. But not dangerous.

"I wanted to be the first to let you know," Nick continued. "We'll be docking in about forty-four hours, and when we arrive, Max will be escorted off the ship and brought to the police station for questioning."

"Thank you…for telling me," Kat said.

"I hope you feel better soon," Nick said. "Let me know if you need anything at all. I'm afraid I need to get back." He left the room, and Kat met Sam's eyes.

"How you doing?" Sam asked.

"I'm okay."

"Brave words."

Kat smiled. "If I say them enough, I may start to believe them."

"I guess our questions are answered," Sam said.

"I guess so. I never would have thought Max could do something like this, though."

"You couldn't have known," Sam said gently. "Guys like him are clever. They're masters at psychological manipulation. It probably started innocently enough. He wanted you back, but when he couldn't sway you, it turned into an obsession."

"Why, though? The explosion could have killed me."

"The guy's not exactly what I would call stable. He was obsessed with the article he was working on. He probably planted the bomb to give himself something to report on. And when people like this get obsessed, it can become deadly."

Kat shivered, wondering if she had simply never really known Max for who he was. "I wonder how he got the explosive on board."

"How do a dozen people disappear each year from cruise ships with no evidence on any security footage? When someone wants something bad enough, they figure out a way."

"I guess you're right."

Sam searched her face, pulled a stool up next to her. "You don't look convinced. What are you thinking?"

"The explosion could have killed me," she said. "Max wouldn't even kill a spider when we were dating. He stopped on the side of the road to help an injured kitten once."

"That doesn't mean anything, Kat," Sam said, but he looked thoughtful, and she knew he wasn't discounting her concerns.

"Maybe not," she said. "But with Morgan missing, I keep going back to that last day, that look on her face. If it wasn't about her brother, then something else must have happened. I keep thinking...something's wrong on this cruise ship, and what if Max is just an easy scapegoat?"

She detected skepticism in his expression, and she sighed, not even sure of her own thoughts at the moment. "You're probably thinking I'm just swayed by him somehow because we dated for a long time."

"No," Sam said. "You're too smart for that. I'm thinking you know Max better than anyone on this cruise ship. If you really don't think he's the guy, then maybe we should still be looking."

Just the knowledge that Sam was hearing her, that he could see merit in her concerns, made Kat feel better.

"I'll talk to Nick about it." He reached over and brushed her hair back from her forehead. "You look tired."

Kat's eyes drifted shut at his caress. "I guess I am," she murmured, lulled by the sudden heavy tug of sleep.

"There's not even a TV in here. Do you want me to go up and grab you a book or something?"

"No, that's okay," she said. "I'm about falling asleep anyway. But maybe you could bring me my cell phone and charger. I want to see if there's any news on Morgan."

"Sure," Sam said. "I'll bring it down to you in a bit. Get some rest." His knuckles skimmed Kat's cheek in a tender goodbye, and the room darkened as he left. She didn't have the energy to ask him to leave a light on, just let him take over all her worries and gave herself up to the draw of sleep.

Sam had known Kat would be surprised when she heard about Max's detainment, but he also thought she'd be relieved. Instead, her response had raised red flags. Nick wouldn't appreciate the news, but Sam was determined to take Kat's concerns seriously. He hoped to get Nick to agree to post a guard by Kat again until they docked.

He jogged down the stairs to deck four and down the hall to the offices, where he found Nick alone, scrolling through security footage. Sam tapped on the open door, and Nick glanced back. "Come on in," he said. "And close the door, would you?"

Sam pulled the door shut and grabbed a chair next to Nick, peering at the monitor as the officer cycled through screen shots.

"I wanted to look through the footage in and around the atrium myself," Nick said.

"You worried you've missed something?"

Nick stopped what he was doing and looked Sam in the eye. Stress was beginning to show in the shadows under his eyes, the rumpled uniform and pale draw of his face. "We're missing some footage."

"What do you mean?"

"Look." Nick pulled up a clip. "Remember the footage I showed you and Kathryn from the corridor on deck ten? This is another one from another camera near the elevators, also deck ten. Watch the time stamp."

Sam watched as the clip rolled, and whistled low. "Four minutes skipped. So why leave the other footage untouched?"

"Oversight, maybe?" Nick suggested. "The camera

didn't catch much. Maybe the perp was in a hurry, missed the footage."

"And you just found this?"

Nick nodded, face grave. "No one else could find anything. I decided to have a look for myself."

"Someone on your team, then."

Nick's mouth folded into a frown. "I don't want to believe it, but the evidence is pointing in that direction."

"And what? Framed Max?"

Nick raised an eyebrow. "He could have easily slipped her that drug. Could have been the one in her room."

Sam shook his head. "I'm thinking it's unlikely we've got two unrelated attacks going on here. Not to mention, how could Max get access?"

"Point taken, but we can't discount Max, especially considering the GHB in his cabin."

"Who else?"

Nick leaned forward and rubbed his forehead, his anxiety palpable. "I'm looking at my list. I've got eleven guys. I've worked with four of them for years, personally brought them to the team on this ship. I don't think it's one of them."

"Okay, so let's start with that. Who did you bring onto the team?"

"Bailey, Moore, Larsen and Byrnes."

"I've never trusted your man Larsen. But I haven't had much contact with the others."

Nick looked at him, surprised. "Tom's my top man, Sam. We started working together almost seven years ago. I've taken him onto my team twice now since my promotion a couple years ago."

"Just a feeling," Sam said. "Let's run through the other names on the list. What's the ETA on the navy ship?"

Nick sighed. "Nine p.m."

"We've managed this long," Sam said. "And I'm thinking you should keep someone guarding Kat. Just in case. But do me a favor and leave Larsen out of it."

Someone was chasing her. Kat ran blindly, fear in her throat. Mouth open, trying to scream. No sound would come. A long, black tunnel, footsteps echoing behind her, breath heaving. Her pulse thundered, and she felt him closing in, the rush of movement gaining speed behind her. She ran faster, lungs burning, away from the shadow in the dark.

A burst of flame, right in front of her. Fire!

Kat's eyes flew open, and she blinked into the darkness, heard a click. Did the door just close? She shot up in bed, searched the room with her eyes. No one was there.

Her pulse raced, hair damp against her neck. Sweat and fear. Her eyes adjusted to the dark, found the cell phone Sam had left on the table next to her bed. She reached for it with a shaky hand.

Just a bad dream, she knew, but the burst of flame had seemed so real. So bright. And what was the clicking sound she'd heard?

She looked at her phone. She was shocked she had slept most of the day away. It was already nearly seven.

She dialed into her voice mail, praying for good news from Lillian Foster. There wasn't any. Police hadn't located Morgan yet, and Lillian hadn't heard from her, either.

I wonder where you are, she thought. *Please, be okay.*

But she was beginning to believe that something terrible had happened to her best friend.

They'd been close for years, but their traveling lifestyles usually kept them apart. The cruise gig had been the perfect way to reconnect. They would sneak down to the empty theater some nights and play music together, Kat on the piano, and Morgan either singing or playing a flute they'd dug up in a room full of old props.

When they were little, they'd dreamed of traveling the world together, performing in grand concert halls. But money was always tight for the Fosters, and Morgan dropped out of college the first year to take on a full-time job.

Kat wondered about the extra money Morgan was receiving. Was it really from work, or had she figured out another way to bring in some extra income? She'd never let on that she needed anything. Kat would have helped her.

She shook her head. She'd make herself crazy with all these questions. What she needed was to get out of the infirmary and into some fresh air.

She dialed Sam, and he picked up immediately. "Hey, Kat," he said warmly. "I've checked on you a couple of times, but you were out. Has the doctor okayed you to leave?"

"Not that I know of," she said. "But I'm feeling ready."

"I'll be right down, see what I can do."

Less than five minutes passed before Sam knocked and entered the room. "It's dreary in here," he said, flipping on the overhead light. He'd showered and shaved, donned dark jeans and wore a sky-blue shirt that lightened his eyes and made him seem more relaxed. "The doctor will be in soon to give you the okay," he said.

"Thanks," Kat said. "Don't feel obligated to stay with me," she added.

Sam pulled over a stool and sat next to her. "My grandmother and her friends are taking a dip in the hot tub."

Kat grinned at the image. "And you don't want to join them?"

"I'll join them when you do."

Kat laughed, a blush creeping up her neck, and Sam laughed, too.

"I think they have bowling on the agenda again for tomorrow afternoon. Maybe that'd be more up your alley."

"If I'm feeling good, sure. I'm warning you, I've got a mean curve ball."

"We'll just see," Sam said, a glint in his eyes. Then he suddenly looked more serious. "I went down to talk to Nick."

"And?"

"He found several minutes of missing footage from cameras near the atrium. He's looking for more."

"So…it would have to be someone from Security," Kat said, thinking out loud.

"The bomb at least, and I'd argue it was the same person in your room both times—the one who unzipped your bag and the one who was on your balcony. But it's still possible Max was responsible for drugging you."

"I don't think—"

"It's *possible*," he said. "That's all I'm saying. But we're looking at other possibilities, too."

"For example?"

"Nick and I sat together and created a list of security team members and anyone else you've had contact with— your cabin steward, Johann, even the captain. My brother's pulling some strings to get some background checks run, trying to get police overseas to cooperate. In the meantime, Nick is still looking through surveillance, and help is still on the way. Plus, you'll have a guard again. Oh, and no more performances. The captain has agreed to keep the theaters closed until we dock."

Kat smiled, relieved. "It sounds like you two are covering all your bases." But then a thought occurred to her, and she frowned. "If it's possible someone on the security team is crooked, then it's not a good thing that they're all armed right now."

Sam grimaced. "Nick and I were discussing that a few minutes ago. He thinks it's safest to keep the force armed, knowing that most of his team is loyal. If they discover the threat, they're better off with an armed team against one armed perpetrator than they would be with an *un*armed team against a perpetrator who may have already built another explosive."

"I see the reasoning, but I'm just thinking—"

Dr. Henry walked in through the adjoining door then and approached Kat, a kind smile on his face. "You're looking much better, Ms. Brooks," he said. "How are you feeling?"

"Normal again," she said, and he nodded with satisfaction.

"Good. Go ahead and try out a walk across the room before I let you go."

Kat swung her legs over the bed, hastily tugging at the hem of her dress as it rode up. Her bare feet hit cold tile, and a chill swept up her nape. But she was sturdy on her feet, only felt a little light-headed. She wasn't about to admit to that, though. She wanted out of this dark room and all its quiet.

"Okay, then," Dr. Henry said. "Looks like you're good to go."

"Thank you for everything," Kat said, slipping her feet into the heels near her bed.

"Take care," the doctor said. "And come back at any time if you start feeling worse."

Sam opened the door for her. "You need some fresh air and sunlight," he said as they walked toward the elevators.

"I've slept most of the day away. Is the sun even up?"

"We can catch it setting if we hurry," he said.

They stepped onto the top deck and into the balmy evening. Kathryn took a long breath of fresh air and a feeling of peace washed over her despite all the unanswered questions. She slipped off her heels and held on to them as Sam led her around to a set of lounge chairs facing the sunset and its brilliant oranges and deep pinks.

Sam started to sit.

"I think I'd like to walk for a bit," Kat said. She'd been lying down for hours, and it felt good to move around.

"I should have thought of that," Sam said. "I'm sure you were restless. Here." He reached over and took her heels, tucking them under his arm.

"Quiet up here," Kat said as they walked leisurely, summer wind blowing her hair back from her face.

"I prefer it to the madness below," Sam said, and Kat smiled.

"What will Alice do after the hot tub?" she asked.

"She and her friends plan to watch a movie in Ann's room."

"I'm surprised you're letting her out of your sight."

He raised an eyebrow, and Kat burst into laughter. "I guess it would be a little creepy sitting by the hot tub with Alice and her girlfriends."

Sam laughed softly. "She promised she would be extra careful."

They turned a corner, and Kat caught sight of a couple down near the end of a row of lounge chairs. The woman curled against the man's side. He stroked her hair and shoulder, and the image drew forth an ache Kat hardly recognized. She looked away, remembering the touch of Sam's lips on her skin.

"You look deep in thought."

Kat blushed, stealing a glance at him, assuring herself he couldn't possibly have read her mind. "Just processing, I guess."

"You okay?"

She nodded. But nothing that had happened was okay. Not her dad's death. Not the house burning to the ground.

Not Morgan's disappearance, and certainly not Max's actions—if he was even guilty of anything.

But here she was, breathing in fresh air, watching a sunset, one sailing day away from the Canary Islands. Walking next to a man who put to shame every romance novel Morgan had ever loaned her.

"You've been through a lot," Sam said. He looked out onto the water. "Grandma always likes to remind me that after every sunset is the chance to see a new sunrise."

Kat moved toward the railing, watched as clouds began to roll in. The sun had nearly disappeared, leaving fading colors in its wake. Funny how she had watched the changes but couldn't pinpoint when they had occurred.

Much like her place in life. She could see those pivotal memories in her mind's eye—holding her mother's hand as she took her last breaths, stepping onto her first international stage as a teenager, standing at the pulpit eulogizing her father. She could see those moments, the ones that had shaped her. But where did it all leave her?

Alone.

Fading into darkness like the remnants of the sun. She could almost see her mother's face, kind gentle eyes looking back at her.

There is always light, Kat. You have to stay right in the center of it. Don't get trapped in the darkness.

She'd tried. She'd tried so hard. Grasping every opportunity, chasing after success. It had all been a trick of the world. Experience and sights masquerading as light. But what she wanted, what she hadn't realized she'd wanted, was family. A lasting love and companionship.

When she'd come back home to take care of her dad, she'd felt so out of touch with her life. Simple things like making beds and cooking meals held more meaning than all of the concerts she'd done in the past year put together.

Because she was doing it all for her father. And she'd missed out on that togetherness.

A prayer whispered silent in her heart for protection from whatever darkness seemed to be closing in, and for direction for her future.

Her gaze fell on Sam, took in his strong profile, wondered if he was part of that. She hoped he was. But regardless, she knew God would make all things new. He could turn ashes to beauty. She just needed to trust.

Such a simple act, yet the hardest of them all.

FIFTEEN

The orange glow was gone, leaving only waning violet and pale gray in its wake. It would soon give way to the rest of the midnight-blue sky beckoning for darkness and sleep.

"Looks like a storm's coming," Sam said, the warmth of his breath soft against her ear, his hand slipping around her waist. Kat's breath hitched. She hadn't realized how close he was.

"I was planning an early night anyway," she said, then turned to him. "Thank you…for everything. If you hadn't been there last night, I'm not sure—"

He stopped her words with the pad of his finger on her lips, and the heat in his gaze sent a swirl of hope firing through her senses.

"I'm just glad you're safe," he said.

And then he dropped his hand and did what she'd been craving all day.

Strong arms gathered around her, and she did the only thing she could. She held on, pressed her face into the solid warmth of his chest, felt the gentle whisper of his lips at her temple, his hand on her back.

"There's something about you," he whispered. "Something that tempts me to make all sorts of promises." He pulled back, troubled eyes meeting hers. "I don't have the kind of life that I can share with someone else, Kat. I don't work nine to five. I miss more holiday functions than I attend. My work is filled with risk, and it demands every part of who I am."

"Not every part," she responded. Her words sounded breathless, even to her own ears. "You're here with your grandmother, watching out for her."

"Under duress," he muttered, and she laughed.

"You know, I miss holidays, too, and more birthdays than I can count…but does it really matter when people care about each other?"

"Sometimes," he said, and Kat's heart broke at the regret in his eyes. "Sometimes it matters more than you could have ever imagined."

She knew he was referring to his wife, how his presence may have been able to prevent her death.

"But, sometimes, I think we fool ourselves into believing that it matters more than it really does," she said. "When my mom died, my dad threw himself into his work, and I secluded myself with the piano. We lived separate lives for years until he got sick, and then we only had a short time together before he passed away…but despite all the time and distance that came between us, our bond never changed."

She wanted to say so much more.

Thank you for saving my life.

Thank you for protecting me.

Kiss me.

A smile rose involuntarily at that idea, but she pressed her lips together, willing away her fanciful thoughts.

Sam caught the curve of Kat's lips, the smile that held a happy secret, and he couldn't help himself. He drew her closer, brushed his lips to hers, tasted the sweetness he'd imagined he'd find.

She sighed and slipped her hands up over his shoulders, and Sam knew he should pull away, but he didn't want to. Not when her hair smelled like vanilla and honeysuckle, and her hands were warm behind his neck and her lips were pliant and welcoming under his.

"Excuse me." A loud voice nearby put a stop to the kiss anyway, and Sam reluctantly pulled away, noted the deep pink in Kat's cheeks. He turned and saw Officer Larsen, looking predictably irritated.

The officer directed his attention to Kat. "Ms. Brooks, we've received communication from the police in Salvador de Bahia."

Kat stiffened at his side, and Sam slipped his hand around hers.

"Your friend still hasn't been located, but the police have found some items they believe may belong to her. We were asked to have you look at a set of photos to see if you recognize anything."

Sam heard Kat take in a trembling breath, saw the well of tears pooling in her eyes.

"Isn't this something Morgan's mother would be doing?" he asked the officer.

"She's on a flight to Brazil as we speak, and they want to keep the case moving forward."

"Show me," Kat said, and Larsen turned on his heel, leading them away to news Sam was sure didn't bode well for Kat's friend.

Nick was standing outside the conference room with Officer Byrnes when Kat and Sam arrived with Officer Larsen.

"I believe you've met Officer Byrnes already," Nick said. "He'll be watching out for you until Officer Moore takes on the day shift tomorrow morning."

Byrnes smiled kindly as Kat and Sam followed the

other officers into the room. Nick gestured for Kat to take a seat at the oval conference table, and her heart pounded a heavy beat as she took the chair Sam pulled out for her. He stood behind her, set a hand on her shoulder, and Kat waited, eyes hot with building tears.

"Officer Larsen has been in contact with the police in Salvador de Bahia regarding your friend," Nick said. "Tom, you want to bring up those pictures?"

Officer Larsen sat across from Kat and touched a few keys on the computer. She didn't want to see the pictures, didn't want proof that Morgan wasn't simply lost in a foreign city or stuck in a shutdown airport.

Even though she already knew.

She wanted to keep hoping and believing her friend was okay.

Larsen's expression softened considerably as he turned the laptop to face her. "I'm sorry I don't have better news to share with you." Genuine sympathy coming from a gruff guy like Larsen started the flow of tears Kat had been desperately holding back.

A delicate gold anklet, Morgan's.

"It's hers," she said, throat aching and heart empty. The familiar pang of loss tore at her heart, and she buried her face in her hands, shoulders heaving with grief.

What had happened to Morgan? Why had she left the ship, if not to go home? And why hadn't she told Kat the real reason?

They'd shared all their secrets since Kat's first day of third grade at Rosings Elementary School in Miami, Florida. Kat's family had just moved to the city so her father could be closer to his work as the state's attorney. Unsure of herself, Kat had walked through the cafeteria that first day, anxiously looking for a place to sit.

Morgan had waved at her. Moved her lunch box over to make room at the table. Reached into her bag.

"I snuck an extra cookie when Mom went to work," she said slyly. *"Want one?"*

Kat sucked in a trembling breath at the memory. She hated this. Hated the ache that came, the emptiness that could never be filled.

"Are you sure?" Larsen pressed, and Kat nodded, drawing in a deep breath, gaining control over her tears.

"I gave it to her...years ago." She stared at the anklet, could see Morgan's reaction as if it were yesterday. It was the day Morgan had set out for her first job cruising.

"It's not too late to change your mind," Kat said as they stood in the parking lot with watery eyes.

"Are you kidding me?" Morgan said with her typical bravado. *"There's no going back now!"*

"Well, in that case..." Kat pulled out the little box and handed it to her best friend.

Morgan opened the box and took out the anklet, its tiny hand-stamped pendant glimmering in the spring sunshine. The imprint of an anchor and a Bible reference. Psalm 139:5.

"Are you going to make me look this up?"

Kat shrugged. "If you don't, you'll never know what it means."

Morgan laughed. "That's one way to get me to open a Bible," she said. *"Very clever."*

"'You hem me in, behind and before,'" Kat whispered. "'You lay your hand upon me.'"

"The Bible verse?" Sam asked gently.

She nodded. "Ironic," she said, and even she didn't like the bitter tone in her voice.

She looked at Larsen, braced herself for another picture. "You said there was more?"

"Just two more," he said and moved to change the photo, but as he reached down, Officer Callahan's radio beeped.

"This is Officer Bailey, looking for Sam West. Respond if you have his location."

Nick pulled his radio out of his belt, eyed Sam. "This is Callahan. Sam West is with me in Conference Room B."

"Report to him that his grandmother took a fall. We're taking her to the infirmary."

Sam let go of Kat's shoulders and looked down at her, worry creasing his brow.

"Go," she said. "I need to be here, and you need to be there."

"I know you're right," he said, then to Nick, "After the meeting, will you walk her up?"

Nick nodded. "Absolutely."

Larsen closed the photo as Sam left the room. The officer clicked on another file. Kat steeled herself, all the while praying that Alice was okay. Sam's grandmother was in good shape, but a simple fall for a woman in her seventies could easily be serious.

"This one?" Larsen asked, and the second photo appeared.

A small brown backpack. It could have been anyone's. Except that it had been found with Morgan's anklet, and Morgan owned a backpack just like it. Had taken it with her the day she left the ship.

Kat nodded, and she was tempted to stand up and say she'd had enough. That she couldn't look at one more thing of her friend's. But she owed it to Morgan to look, to make sure. To help the police in any way she could.

"Callahan, this is Officer Jameson." A female voice came through Nick's radio. "We have a situation in the security office. Several of our cameras are down."

Nick's brow furrowed, and he jumped up. "On my way," he said. He directed his attention to Kat. "Byrnes will walk you to the infirmary when you're through here. I'm sorry about your friend. Let me know if I can do anything…"

He couldn't. No one could. But Kat thanked him anyway as he left the room.

Larsen stood, as well.

"Do you need to get to that, too?" Kat asked. "I can come back later."

He shook his head. "No. I'll just be a minute," he said. "Sit tight."

He left the room, the image of Morgan's backpack staring back at Kat. She folded her arms on the table and laid her head down, wondering how much loss she would have to bear in this life.

Her cell phone vibrated, and she reached into her jeans pocket to retrieve it. She saw the text floating at the top of her screen, and every muscle froze.

Kat, this is Morgan. I'm okay. Please tell me you are, too.

Kat's heart beat hard against the wall of her chest, and she called the number Morgan was texting from.

Her friend picked up on the first ring.

"Kat?" Morgan's voice was loud and strung with emotion. "I'm so glad you're okay. I saw a picture... What happened? Were you in the hospital?"

"What picture? Where *are* you?"

"Don't worry about me. I'm in a cab, and I'll be at the American Embassy soon. I'm okay. But you're not safe, Kat."

"What's going on, Morgan?" Kat whispered, the hairs at the nape of her neck rising.

"Didn't you find my note?"

"No...what note?"

"It doesn't matter now. Listen, Kat, stay away from Officers Larsen and Byrnes. They're dangerous. I think there are others, but I don't know who."

Kat leaped up from her seat. "What do you mean?" she

asked, hurrying to the door. She'd run up to the infirmary and get as far away from the officer as she could.

"I'm so sorry, Kat," Morgan said. "It's all my fault."

Kat reached for the door. "What? *What's* all your fault?"

She pulled the door open and came face-to-face with Officer Larsen.

He motioned back to the room, filled the doorway, leaving her no space to slide past him.

"Sorry about that," he said.

Kat didn't budge. "I'm just going to take this phone call," she offered, trying to steady her voice. Larsen's eyes narrowed, and he glanced at the cell phone pressed to her ear.

They stood inches apart.

"I shouldn't have gotten involved," Morgan continued. "But I was just trying to—"

Larsen reached forward and yanked the phone out of Kat's hand, put it to his ear.

Kat lunged forward, tried to squeeze past him, but with one hard shove, he knocked her back into the room. Kat stumbled, jarring into the edge of the table.

Larsen kicked the door shut behind him, listening to Morgan.

"Too late," he said into the phone, and in one swift motion, he pulled the cover off and dropped the phone onto the floor, smashing it with a solid boot on hard tile. Kat's blood went cold.

"Before you do anything you'll regret, like scream—" Larsen reached a hand into his pocket and pulled out a black device that fit in the palm of his hand "—remember what happened in the atrium?"

She stared at him, every muscle on edge.

"Remember?" he prodded, a dangerous tone to his voice, and Kat nodded.

"Would be a shame if that happened again. In the infirmary."

Kat didn't dare move, her eyes fixed on the rectangular device the officer held.

"The button in the center. Hold it down for five seconds. That's all it will take. Unless you give me what I want."

He slipped the device back into his pocket and pulled out a piece of paper, shoving it across the table at Kat.

It was a memo sheet torn from a pad in a guest room. A hastily scrawled note.

Did you get my note? That was what Morgan had asked her. No, she hadn't. Larsen had. But how? She scanned the letter, dread heightening.

> Kat, in case something happens to me, I left something for you in a place only you'll know—REMEMBER OUR CHILDHOOD DREAMS. Go get it. If you haven't heard from me in twenty-four hours, you'll know what to do. Love, Morgan
> P.S. Be careful no one sees you. There are dangerous people on this ship.

Fear settled in Kat's chest and she could hear her own rapid breaths in the stillness of the room.

Their dreams...*the flute.*

"Where did you get this?"

"You have a clever friend," Larsen said. "Pinned it inside that blue dress of yours."

The garment bag. Larsen had been in her room. Searching it.

"It's a good thing the chandelier missed you after all. Turns out you're of more use to us alive than dead. For now."

"How? I don't know anything about—"

Larsen held up a hand, and the words died on Kat's lips.

"We saw you two together," he said knowingly. "All that crying and carrying on before she tried to run. We know you know."

Kat shook her head, opened her mouth to insist she didn't, but a vicious cold had filled his eyes, and she kept her mouth shut.

"First, you're going to pick up your broken cell phone for me."

He hovered over the cell phone, holding the detonator, and Kat could do nothing but comply. She picked up the broken pieces of her phone and passed them into Larsen's hand, stepping away from him quickly.

He dropped the parts into his pocket.

"Good," he said, an erratic light in his eyes. "Now we're going to take a little walk." He knew he had her. "You have exactly ten minutes to find what your friend left on ship, or you'll have a lot of blood on your hands." He pinched a button on his watch and it beeped. "Starting now."

Kat's heart lurched. She had no choice. She'd take him there, and she'd try to escape afterward, try to warn Sam, or figure out a way to get the detonator away from Larsen.

She stood taller, willed herself to appear braver than she felt.

Larsen moved to open the door, looked down at her. "One wrong move, one wrong word, and I press that button."

Kat hesitated.

Would he really? After all, if he did, he'd be caught. Kat would tell…unless he silenced her first. He was a muscular man and could easily overpower her.

"Time's ticking," he said, and Kat stepped out into the hallway.

"That's a girl," Larsen added, and she wanted to throw up. "Now tell me where we're going."

* * *

Sam took the stairs two at a time to reach deck five, raced around the corner and down the hall to the infirmary. Prayed the whole way that his grandmother was okay.

Officer Bailey stood outside the door with Grandma's friends.

It wasn't a pretty sight.

The three grandmothers were dripping wet, water pooling at their bare feet, too-small towels pulled tight around themselves, gaping in all the wrong places. Thinning wet hair matted to scalps, shivering.

"They found you," Ann said. "I'm so glad!"

Sam reached for the door and yanked the handle. Locked. He pounded.

"Dr. Henry said to tell you he'd come get you in a few minutes," Ann said gently. "They're changing Alice into something dry so she can warm up."

"Is she okay?" Sam asked. "What happened?"

"She'll be okay, Sammy," Norah said, and he wanted to tell her that only his grandmother was allowed to call him that, but he held himself back. "What happened?" he repeated.

"We had just gotten out of the hot tub, and she slipped and fell," Ann said.

"Hit her head, bam!" Dottie added. "She blacked out, and we all went into a tizzy."

"She blacked out?"

"Only for a few seconds, but when she got up, she was dizzy and felt sick. We got this kind young man to bring us a wheelchair and find you." She gestured to Officer Bailey, and the man smiled, held out a hand.

"Pleased to meet you," Bailey said.

"And you," Sam said, then turned to Grandma's friends. "You ladies should get warm and dry, too," he said. "I'll wait here, and you can come back when you're dressed."

"I'm staying with Alice," Dottie said, a determined look on her face.

"I'm afraid I am, too," Ann agreed, though her lips were nearly blue from the cold.

"Looks like they're determined," the officer said, amusement playing across his face.

Sam sighed. Stubborn ladies, just like his grandmother. "Thanks for getting ahold of me."

"Sure thing," Bailey said. "I hope it all turns out okay. I need to get back to the office. Keep me posted."

The officer headed away from the infirmary, and Sam paced outside the door, checking his watch every minute while his grandmother's friends pretended not to notice.

"How long does it take to get dressed?" Sam said after a solid ten minutes had passed.

"Well, now, bathing suits are a tricky thing," Dottie said.

"Especially wet bathing suits," said Ann.

"On wrinkly old ladies," Norah added, and they all giggled nervously.

The door opened, and Sam was grateful in more ways than one.

"You may come in now," Nurse Sutter said.

His grandmother was lying on the bed, the same bed Kat had been in hours ago. Hair wrapped in a towel and blankets pulled up to her chin, skin as pale as the white sheets. All three of her friends hurried over, clinging to their towels.

"Grandma?"

She squinted her eyes opened, but shut them quickly. "Too much light," she said.

Sam leaned down and kissed her forehead, then moved to turn off the overhead light.

He looked at the nurse. "Is she okay?"

She smiled reassuringly. "Dr. Henry is writing up his assessment. This definitely looks like a concussion and—"

The adjoining door opened and Dr. Henry walked in. "Glad they found you," he said to Sam. "You're grandmother fell getting out of the hot tub, and she's suffered a grade-three concussion. We'll keep her here to recover."

"How serious is it?"

"She should be just fine," the doctor said. "But it will take a while before she regains her balance and all her faculties. She took quite a fall."

Sam reached over, tucked the blanket higher under his grandmother's chin, and she peeked her eyes open again.

"Looks like trouble really does seem to follow me," she said, and he didn't like the weak tone of her voice. "But I didn't fall like they're saying." She crooked a finger at him, and he leaned close so she could whisper in his ear.

"I was pushed."

For a split second, Sam wondered if it was the concussion talking, but he saw the fear in his grandmother's eyes, and a sick feeling took root in his gut.

"Kat," he said, and his grandmother nodded.

"Go, Sammy. Find her."

He turned and ran, the door slamming back as he threw it open.

He called Kat on the way, but her phone went straight to voice mail. Had someone pushed his grandmother to get Kat alone?

Larsen.

SIXTEEN

Deck six was packed, and Kat watched the faces of passengers and crew, hoping someone's eyes would light on hers, praying she'd have a chance to let someone know she needed help—without Larsen catching her. But before her, the doors to the Topaz Theater stood solid and foreboding, and no one seemed to be paying any attention to Kat walking toward them, Larsen several paces behind.

Kat shivered, opened the first set of doors and braced herself against the dark. Hastily, she opened the second set and stepped into the theater, a blanket of black quiet surrounding her.

"Hold on a minute." Larsen's voice came gruffly behind her, and he turned on a flashlight, pointing it down the aisle. "Move."

There are dangerous people on this ship.

Larsen was one of them. And Byrnes. Were there others?

They reached the top of the aisle, and Larsen said, "Six minutes, forty-five seconds."

Kat ran up the steps to the stage and crossed toward the back. She would get in there, find whatever it was she needed and get out. She had to find a way.

It was the last room along the back wall. That was

where the old props were kept. She let herself in, Larsen right behind her, and flipped on the lights.

She blinked against the brightness, felt the urgency building. She needed to move faster. What if Larsen detonated the bomb anyway? He could. Easily. But would he? If he had everything he was looking for?

"Four minutes, thirty seconds."

Kat rushed over to the locked drawers. She reached under the cabinet for the key, then unlocked the bottom drawer and pulled it out. The metal slid loudly, and she looked down into the drawer. It stored two flutes, a clarinet and an oboe. They'd been used as props in a show in the past. As far as she knew, no one used them anymore. She grabbed the flutes, set them in her lap. Took out the other instruments. Laid them on the floor next to her. Looked in the drawer.

Nothing.

Alarmed, she peered all around the inside and underneath the drawer. Surely this was what Morgan had meant? Or maybe she'd meant the piano.

Frustrated, knowing she was wasting precious time, she quickly put the clarinet and oboe back, then grabbed the flute Morgan had played. She examined it for any clues, turned it over, peered inside. Was that paper stuffed inside?

She grabbed a pencil from the desk and made quick work of bringing the paper out toward her. There. The corner of the paper hung out of the flute. She grabbed it and tugged gently. It was snug. She tugged again, willing it not to rip.

Slowly, she shimmied the paper out. Heard a clink.

A tiny green rock sparkled on the tile floor at her feet. Kat leaned down to get a closer look, and several more trickled to the floor.

The paper had been carefully wrapped. She unwrapped

it gently and saw several more of the pretty green stones. Jewels? Roughly cut. Emeralds?

Her heart pounded in her chest. Cold fear enveloped her as she focused on the words Morgan had written to her. The note was dated four weeks ago, on their last cruise.

Kat,
I hope you never have to read this, but if you do, I'm sorry. I—

"Give it to me," Larsen said, voice low and dangerous. He held the remote in his hand, thumb poised over the center.

Fear consumed her. Frantically, Kat scooped the gems into her palm. She wanted to read Morgan's note, but she didn't have time.

Carefully, she set the handful of stones in the note, folded it back up and walked over to Larsen. She reached forward to deposit the treasures into his empty hand, but her eyes lit on the remote again.

She wondered if she could get it away from him. Make a run for it, screaming at the top of her lungs for help.

It was worth a try.

Kat set the packet in Larsen's hand and then jumped toward his other hand, tried to grab the remote. He swiped his hand away and made a tsking sound, as if to tease her. But his eyes held no humor.

"You shouldn't have done that," he said.

"You have what you wanted," Kat said. "Let me go."

Larsen smiled. It was a smile that sent stark cold fear spiraling deep into Kat's gut. "Not so fast." He palmed the remote and grabbed her arm, fingers digging painfully into muscle.

"You're coming with me."

* * *

Sam raced down the stairs toward the security offices, dread building with every step he took.

He'd let down his defenses, and now he was staring into the face of what he'd been running from for two years: failure.

He burst into the conference room, but it was empty. Just as he'd suspected it would be. He ran down the hall to the security office and barged in without knocking. The three officers inside jumped, turned to him.

"Does anyone know where Callahan is?" Sam asked.

"Meeting with the captain," Officer Moore said.

"I need him now!" Sam yelled. "It's an emergency!"

The officer pulled out her radio. "Callahan, Sam West is asking for you. Says it's an emergency."

"Put him on" came the reply.

Sam took the radio. "Is Kathryn with you?"

"No. Larsen radioed up a bit ago and said Kat needed some time alone," Nick said. "Byrnes escorted her to your grandmother's room. She isn't there?"

Sam knew she wouldn't be there. "I thought we'd agreed you'd stick with her."

"Sam, you need to calm down," Nick said. "We've got a small crew manning a lot of problems right now. I'm doing the best I can. Go check her room. I'll meet you there."

Sam reached the twelfth floor as Nick came off another elevator, and they ran down the hall together.

"She's not answering her phone," Sam said. "Something's wrong."

He pounded on the door when they reached his grandmother's stateroom. He didn't want to barge in on Kat if she was genuinely trying to get some privacy. "Kat! Are you in there?"

No answer.

Nick and Sam exchanged looks, and Sam pulled out the keycard, but Nick held up a hand to stop him.

He bent down and pulled up his pant leg, revealing an ankle holster. "Here," he said, passing the pistol to Sam and then drawing the gun from the holster at his waist.

Nick swiped the key, and Sam barged into the room.

It was empty. Bed tidy, an elephant-shaped towel on Grandma's pillow.

But no Kat.

He hadn't expected her to be there. He turned to Nick, fear welling up and pushing him into action.

"We need to search the ship. Every room."

Nick shook his head. "We can't search every room. Think about the logistics with our manpower. Come on!" He jogged away from the room, and Sam kept pace with him. "Let's get a look at what the cameras picked up."

Sam wasn't holding out hope that the cameras would pick anything up when they had caught so little happening on the ship already.

"How far out is the navy?" Sam asked.

Nick sent him a grim look. "Four hours."

They didn't have four hours to spare. They may already be too late. Every footstep felt leaden with the knowledge, and the fear. First Marissa and their baby.

Please, God, not Kat, too.

"I thought you were going to take her to the infirmary," Sam said.

"I'm sorry, Sam," Nick said. "I was called away. I trusted Byrnes to watch out for her."

"We need to find him."

Nick pointed to the stairs. "Elevator will take too long."

Nick's cell phone rang, and he put it to his ear. "Callahan." He listened as the two ran down the stairwell. "You did the right thing, Sheri," he said. "Sit tight. And see if

you can locate Byrnes or Larsen." He pocketed the phone
and looked over at Sam.

"That was Sheri Moore. Said she just got a phone call.
From Morgan Foster."

All white with a black sign that read Crew Only, a
door loomed before Kat as she walked a few paces in
front of Larsen through a large costume warehouse. It
looked harmless enough, but she knew what lay beyond.
A stairwell that led to crew quarters and into the bowels
of the ship.

*You know how many people go missing off cruises every
year?* Max's voice rang in her mind. If she let Larsen lead
her through that door, she wouldn't have a chance.

But if she didn't go with him, Sam and Alice may not
have a chance.

She had to try. She couldn't just let the man lead her to
certain death. A stepladder leaned against the wall ahead.
Maybe if she grabbed it and swung it at him…

Probably not enough time before he grabbed her.

He had a gun. Maybe he wouldn't risk using it in here.
But maybe he would.

"Faster," Larsen hissed, pushing her forward, and his
radio beeped.

"Officer Larsen, state your location."

Nick Callahan. All she needed to do was alert him that
something was wrong.

Larsen let go of her arm and pulled up his radio. She
eyed the remote in his hand as he waved it at her, a silent
reminder.

"Deck fourteen promenade," he said into the radio.
"Smoke break."

"We're looking for Kathryn Brooks," Nick said, and
Kat's heart leaped. They knew something was wrong.

"She's not in Ms. West's stateroom, and we can't locate Byrnes."

Larsen stared hard at Kat, a warning in his eyes, then radioed back, "Last I saw, that's where she was headed— to her room with Byrnes escorting."

This was her chance, Kat knew. Maybe her only one.

"Report to the security office," Nick said.

"Roger that," Larsen responded. "I'll be—"

"Topaz Theater! Help!" Kat screamed as she lunged forward, taking Larsen by surprise. She hit him squarely in the chest with her body, and he stumbled backward, dropping the radio and grabbing at Kat's arms.

She twisted away, her focus on his left hand, fisted around the remote. She jumped up, tried to grab Larsen's arm, but he was too quick, too strong.

He threw a fist into her cheek, and Kat reeled back, landing on the floor.

Larsen stood over her, eyes blazing anger, and he pocketed the remote.

Kat's head pounded from the blow, and she scrambled back, away from Larsen and his eyes that promised death. Had the remote just been a ploy to get what he wanted? Had she done the wrong thing?

"Larsen! Come in!" The radio blared at the officer's feet.

"You're going to be sorry you did that," Larsen growled and grabbed her by her hair.

Kat screamed, trying to yank out of his grip, but his strength far outmatched hers, and he dragged her toward the backstage crew door. She struggled, grabbing at anything she could fight with, trying desperately to gain traction with her shoes on the smooth floor.

He turned and punched her in the stomach, and all her breath left her. Her legs gave out, and Larsen opened the door and dragged her through.

Kat tried to tear away from him, but she was no match for his strength, and her hands clawed desperately at the door as it slammed shut behind them.

Larsen drew his gun, put it to her temple. "Get up," he muttered.

Kat stood on shaky legs, praying that Nick had heard her on his radio. Larsen forced her down the stairs, gun to her head, and pulled out his cell phone.

"Byrnes," he said, "they're onto us. Meet me in the hold. You'll need to take care of the girl so I can get back upstairs."

He pocketed the cell phone, and Kat stumbled down the stairs in front of him.

Hot tears spilled down her face as she thought of Sam, how he would take all of this on himself. But it was her fault. She shouldn't have gone with Larsen.

She wouldn't.

She stopped and turned toward the security officer, the barrel of the gun near her eye.

He didn't want to kill her here—he knew he'd be caught. Byrnes was waiting to do the job.

"Move!" Larsen said, and a door above them slammed open.

"Kathryn!"

Sam. Coming down the stairs!

Larsen yanked her back, hand fisting painfully in her hair, gun pressed to the side of her head.

Footsteps echoed, fast along the metal steps. Sam turned the corner, weapon drawn.

He met Kat's eyes, and she wondered if this would be their last moment together.

You're too late. Again.

Sam shook the thought away as he stared into Kat's

terrified eyes. Not too late. Just in time. She was alive. For now.

Larsen wore a sneer on his face, eyes wild.

"Get back!" Larsen demanded, and Sam lowered his weapon, but only a little.

He saw murder in the man's eyes, a calm steadiness to the way he held the gun. The officer had nothing to lose at this point, and Sam had everything to lose. "Drop your gun," Larsen commanded, ferocious.

Sam wouldn't do it. He saw the intention. He raised his gun, aimed.

Four gunshots sounded in succession.

Larsen fell backward, his body slamming against the stairs as Kat tried to run up them, away from her attacker.

Blood dripped down the side of her face and along her neck, and she stumbled as Sam closed the distance between them.

He couldn't think about what might have happened to her if he'd arrived a few minutes later. He fought back the self-accusation, the voice telling him he should have known. He should have been quicker. Smarter. More observant.

She was here, now, and she was alive.

"You found me," Kat whispered. Her voice was broken, tears pooling in her eyes.

"We're not out of the woods yet," Sam said. "How do you feel?"

"I'm alive," she said simply. "He's working with Byrnes. He's waiting in the hold."

She reached up to the side of her head, alarm lighting in her expression when she felt the blood.

"It's not yours," Sam said gently, and Kat shivered as he wrapped his arms around her, pulling her close, thanking God that this time he had been there. This time, he wouldn't have regrets.

"It's going to be okay. You ready to get out of here?"

She nodded, her head bumping his chin.

He helped her to her feet, holding fast to her waist as she leaned against him. He needed to get her to safety and quickly. "Almost there," he whispered as the door came into view. But Kat stumbled suddenly, and Sam caught her as she fell forward.

She'd passed out, probably shock. He lifted her into his arms and reached for the door but saw blood on his arm.

Looked down and stopped short.

Blood drenched Kat's left leg. He looked behind them, despair building at the trail of blood. His two shots had both hit Larsen, and he knew Larsen had gotten in two shots as he fell. But Kat had seemed fine.

Only she wasn't. One of Larsen's bullets had hit her in the back of the thigh from the looks of it. She was losing blood fast.

"Don't die on me," he said. Then he begged God, "Don't You let her die on me."

SEVENTEEN

A soft beeping woke Kat, and her eyes flew open. She tried to sit up, but she was attached to something.

The room was dark, a glow coming from the machines at her side and a faint light from around the corner, probably the bathroom. She was in a hospital. An IV protruded from her hand. Her leg ached. She reached down, felt a thick bandage encasing her thigh.

Memories assaulted her. Her cell phone, smashed. Larsen holding out the detonator. His wild eyes, the gun aiming.

Sam.

Her gaze darted around the room until she found him sitting nearby, asleep in a recliner, head back.

"Sam?" she said quietly, and he sat up, reached a hand toward hers, squeezed gently.

"I'm here," he said and looked at Kat with a tenderness that took her breath away.

"You did it again."

"What'd I tell you about my Sammy?"

Startled, Kat looked across the room and finally saw the shadow of Alice sitting in a chair in the corner.

Kat laughed softly, her throat dry and scratchy.

"Where are we?"

"University Hospital," Sam said. "The Canary Islands. You had surgery last night. It was touch-and-go for a while." He moved to sit on the edge of the hospital bed, his thigh brushing hers.

Kat swallowed. She'd escaped death yet again.

"Larsen?" she asked.

"He didn't make it," Sam said, and Kat knew what he meant. She'd seen Sam aiming, his eyes dark and focused, knew he had taken Larsen down in order to save her life.

"Dr. Henry was able to stabilize you, and the navy ship sent a helicopter," Sam explained. "They got you out of there fast. You'd lost a lot of blood."

Kat searched her mind for memories, but the last thing she recalled was Sam raising his gun. "And they let you come with me?" she asked, surprised.

Sam cracked a sheepish smile, and Alice giggled. "First time I've heard my Sammy tell a lie since he was just a boy," Alice said.

"What lie?" Kat asked.

"I said you were my fiancée," he admitted and grinned.

Her heart skipped a beat.

"He's a quick thinker, my Sammy," Alice said. "See what he did with your ring?"

Kat looked down and saw that her mother's wedding band had been moved from her right ring finger to her left.

Sam brushed a hand through his hair. "After everything we'd been through, I couldn't leave you alone," he said. "Sorry about the lie."

"Don't be," Kat said softly. "I'm glad you didn't leave me."

"Grandma lied, too," Sam said, a teasing glimmer in his eyes as he glanced over at Alice.

Alice stood up, grabbed her purse. "I did feel as though a heart attack was coming on," she said. "And, with my age, you can never be too careful."

Kat laughed at Alice's admission, warmth spreading all

over at the thought of two people who had been merely strangers a few days ago going to such great lengths to stay by her side.

"I don't know how to thank you both," Kat said.

"No thanks necessary," Alice said and leaned over Kat's bed to pat her hand. "It was quite an adventure, my girl. And now that I've seen to it that you're okay, I'm going back to the hotel to pack up. I'm sure Sam will fill you in on the rest."

"Pack up?" Kat asked.

"Our flight leaves in a few hours," Sam said.

Regret tugged at the edges of Kat's heart, somewhere deep and forgotten that had long been cold. She didn't feel ready to let Sam go, but she knew she couldn't ask him to stay.

In the months since her father died, Kat had grown weary of her traveling lifestyle, more keenly aware of her lack of community, all the obligations that pulled her away from the people she cared most about. Life was sweeter with people in it, even if you couldn't be sure how long they would be there.

The door creaked shut behind Alice, and Sam slipped his hand over Kat's, his thumb caressing her skin.

"Good news about Morgan," he said quietly.

"She made it to the embassy?"

Sam nodded. "She's a few hours out from Miami now," he said. "She called several times this morning, really wanted to talk to you before she boarded her flight."

"Did she tell you anything?" Kat asked. She was frustrated she'd missed Morgan's call. She wanted to hear her friend's voice and find out what had gone so terribly wrong.

"The extra money she'd been wiring to her mom was pay from a job she'd taken on in April," Sam said. "Transporting illegally mined gemstones to and from the cruise ship."

"A smuggling ring?" Kat couldn't reconcile the truth with what she knew about her friend.

Sam nodded. "She told me that until last week, she'd only transferred cargo out of the ship and to buyers."

"Why would she even get involved in that?" Anger surged, and Kat wanted to talk to Morgan more than ever, to understand why her friend had cast off all her good sense and gotten mixed up with something illegal and dangerous.

"She was pretty distraught about it when she relayed the information to me," Sam said. "Sounds like she felt desperate to help her mom with Jake's medical bills and convinced herself the operation wasn't hurting anyone."

"But?" Kat asked, because she could tell there was a *but*.

"She started to sense she'd gotten in over her head. That's when she hid the emeralds with the note, a kind of insurance, she explained. This last time, her assignment was to bring the cargo from the mining location back to the cruise ship. She saw kids working the mine. At least a dozen. And under horrible conditions. She couldn't justify what she'd done anymore. She wanted out."

"But she was in too deep?"

Sam nodded.

Which was why she'd looked so terrified that last day, and why she'd left without telling Kat the truth.

"She told you all of this?"

Sam shook his head. "No, only some. Nick got ahold of the interview notes, emailed me a copy."

"So she was followed?"

"Yes," Sam said. "That's when she lost her cell phone, when she was running from the men following her. Said it was two men. She hid for several hours, but they caught her and took her to an apartment, waiting on instructions from up the chain of command."

"The chain of command?"

"It was a complex ring of criminals," Sam said. "A couple days later, they started trying to get Morgan to tell them the location of what she'd hidden. She knew they'd intercepted the note but didn't realize you were in any kind of danger."

Kat's mind reeled with the news. "How did she get away?"

Sam shook his head. "I'd like to know myself. Part of the interview is sealed. But I do know someone took a picture of you when you were in the infirmary. It was sent to the cell phone of one of her captors. They showed it to her, a threat, and that's when she said she knew she had to escape."

Kat's heart sank, her imagination running with all the ways Morgan could have managed to escape, spurred on by the desperate need to save Kat's life.

"What happened to Byrnes?"

"He's being held. Police suspect more people on ship, but they're still investigating."

"What about—"

A tap sounded at the door, interrupting Kat's question, and Sam stood. He crossed the small room and cracked the door open. After a momentary exchange of hushed words, he shut the door and turned back to Kat. "Nick Callahan is here with the captain. Want me to tell them you're not up to visitors?"

Yes, she did. But they'd gone out of their way to visit her. "That's okay. I'd like to see them."

He looked as if he might argue, but instead he walked back to the door and opened it. "Come in, guys, but she's pretty tired."

"We won't stay long," Nick said kindly as he stepped into the room ahead of the captain.

They both still wore their uniforms, but neither stood as tall and confident as she'd seen them in the past. Nick spoke first.

"Thanks for seeing us," he started. "I feel responsible for what you've been through. I trusted my men. Guess I got complacent. It almost cost you your life. An apology can't undo your ordeal, but I am sorry." His blue eyes swam with guilt, and Kat shook her head.

"Please don't apologize. You did everything you could. You did all the right things."

"You're kind to say so, Ms. Brooks, but I should have done more." He looked at Sam. "I hope you'll forgive me, too."

"You did what you could, and Kat's alive," Sam said. "I forgive you because you're asking me to, but I really just want to say thank-you. If you'd shut me out, I'm not sure we'd have the same outcome today."

"That means a lot, Sam." Nick turned his attention back to Kat. "Max was released a few hours ago, after a statement from Johann, your cabin steward."

"He approached me as the navy boarded," the captain explained. "He didn't know who to turn to, but guilt was eating at him. Larsen had bribed him to plant the evidence in Max's room. He didn't realize what he was getting mixed up with."

Kat's mind swirled with that new information. She had a thousand questions, and they all wanted to come out at once.

"So someone else must have slipped it into my tea that night. I did leave it at the piano for a few minutes. Wow," she added. "I wouldn't have expected that from Johann."

"I guess when you're overworked and can barely support your family, it's tempting to go the easy way," the captain said. "The entire experience is giving me a new appreciation for staff hours and wages." He moved closer to Kat, shoulders drooped, eyes shadowed with fatigue. "Like Callahan said, I can't make up for what you've been through, but I'd like to release you from the duration of your contract and offer you full compensation."

"Thank you," Kat said, relieved and grateful for the offer. "Somehow I don't see myself going on another cruise ship anytime in the near future."

"No luxury cruise for your honeymoon, then?" Nick asked, eyes twinkling. "Congratulations. I heard you two are engaged."

Kat's gaze flew to her left hand, where the dim light glistened off the surface of her mother's gold wedding band. "No, Sam made it up so they'd let him on the helicopter with me."

Sam's hand slid over hers, and he laughed softly.

Nick and the captain shared a laugh, too, and then began to take their leave.

"I'm glad to see you're okay," Nick said to Kat and then looked at Sam. "Well done."

Sam nodded his thanks. "Likewise."

"It was a pleasure to meet you both," the captain added as the two made their way to the door, and then he looked back, eyes shining. "And should your circumstances change, I'm sure we could arrange a cruise-ship honeymoon that would make you forget everything that happened this week."

Sam left Kat blushing and walked the men to the door as they said their goodbyes. Then he came back to her, sitting on the edge of the hospital bed. Finally, everyone was gone again, and the quiet settled around them.

"What will they do with Morgan?" Kat asked the one question she'd been worrying about since she'd heard the news.

"She's been offered immunity for her testimony," Sam said. "Johann, too."

Relief washed over her. "Some good news, finally." She smiled. "I've never been so happy to be in a hospital bed. On dry land."

"I thought I'd lost you," Sam said.

Kat sucked in a breath, saw the pain in his eyes.

"And I couldn't lose you. In that moment when I saw Larsen aiming his gun, I knew I needed more time with you."

Kat smiled, heart pounding with hope. "Well, I've got a lot of time on my hands."

Sam squeezed her hand. "When you get back, I want you to meet the rest of my family."

"I'd love to," Kat said.

"I was hoping you'd feel that way." Sam smiled, really smiled. Just the way that family photo had captured him, and Kat's heart fluttered, remembering the hopes Alice had confided in her just a few days ago.

I keep praying that God will bring another woman into his life. Someone who can bring back that smile.

Tears stung her eyes as she realized her own prayers had been answered, too. For healing, for direction, for a new start. Her answer couldn't get much clearer than this...

Sam by her side, holding the hand that held her mother's wedding ring. So bent on staying with her that he'd thought to transfer the ring from her right to her left and then weave a spectacular little story that they were engaged.

"Why the tears?" Sam asked, and he brushed a droplet away.

"They're happy ones," Kat said.

"You've had to deal with a lot of loss," he said. "You deserve a happy ending."

He didn't want to leave Kat at the hospital, but he needed to be with his grandmother for the long flight home. And ever since Kat had come through surgery, a feeling of peace had settled over him.

He didn't know why Marissa and Hope were taken so early, and he never would. But he looked at Kat and saw a second chance, a gift.

A memory rose, just a glimpse, of that first day in his new home as an insecure eleven-year-old desperately wanting love, a family, people he could count on…people who could count on him.

"This time, it's going to stick, Sammy," his grandmother said, tender eyes seeking connection with him.

He shrugged. "How do you know?"

"Because God orchestrated it, and He's a God of second chances. He loves new beginnings."

"I hate to go," he said.

"Your grandmother needs you," she assured him, and he knew it was true, even though he wished he could stay.

Sam leaned over Kat, pressed a feathery kiss to her brow, her cheek, the tip of her nose and, finally, her mouth.

"Take care of yourself, Kat," Sam said close to her ear. "And hurry home."

EIGHTEEN

It was over.

That was what Kat was thinking three days later as a passenger assistant wheeled her from the terminal toward baggage claim.

The doctors had wanted her to stay longer, but she'd insisted on leaving. She couldn't withstand one more day recovering at a hospital in a foreign country. She needed to go home.

Even if home meant a temporary apartment for a while.

She spotted Morgan right away, her auburn curls bouncing as she ran to greet Kat, threw her arms around her in the wheelchair and hugged her fiercely.

"You look good!" she said.

"No, I don't." She was actually a mess, dark circles under her eyes, a yellowish bruise on the side of her face, a bandage above her right ear and rumpled clothes.

"You're right. You don't look so hot," Morgan said with a laugh. "But you're alive, so you look pretty good to me!" Her smile fell a little. "I'm so sorry," she said softly.

"You can stop apologizing," Kat said. They'd gotten a chance to speak on the phone the day before, and Morgan had apologized about every ten seconds. "And one thing did come out of it."

Morgan nodded. "That's what I keep trying to remind myself," she said.

And it was true. Morgan's poor choice to sign on with Larsen and his ring had led to help for about twenty children under the age of twelve working in the mines in Salvador de Bahia.

"I've got this," Morgan said to the wheelchair assistant and began to push Kat toward the baggage claim. They passed the first three baggage carousels and turned toward baggage-carousel number four.

And there was Sam.

Wearing dark jeans and a gray oxford shirt that matched the color of his eyes, a broad smile on his face.

Kat's heart danced.

"He wouldn't take no for an answer," Morgan said, parking the wheelchair and leaning close to Kat's ear. "Looks like you have some secrets of your own that I need to hear about right away."

"What are you doing here?" Kat asked.

Sam laughed. "It's good to see you, too."

He looked good. Better than good. He looked like a million dreams woven together in one breath.

"I thought you might need a ride."

"She did, since you told me I couldn't drive her," Morgan said with a grin.

"You look beautiful."

Kat laughed.

He bent close. "You laugh, but you are beautiful, Kat." He kissed her temple and straightened. "Tell me when you see your luggage. I'll grab it."

Minutes later, Sam wheeled Kat out of the airport and into the breezy summer evening as Morgan walked close at her side.

She breathed in the fresh air. "I was expecting humidity. This is refreshing."

"Storms came through yesterday, cooled everything down," Sam said.

He wheeled her toward the parking lot and stopped at a black SUV. Piled her two suitcases and a pair of crutches into the back, then leaned down to help her into the vehicle while Morgan climbed into the back.

"You must be exhausted," he said to Kat as he climbed into the driver's seat and rolled down the windows.

"A bit," she said. "But I feel pretty good. I slept most of the last flight back."

Sam put the SUV in Reverse and headed toward the exit. He glanced over at Kat. "In that case, and don't feel pressured, but you're invited to dinner at my grandmother's house. I'm warning you, though. The whole family will be there."

Kat's mind raced. He was inviting her to meet his family. She knew this must be big, and she couldn't help the smile forming on her lips. "I'd love to go."

Sam reached a hand over, caressing the back of her neck. "I was hoping you'd say that." He glanced at Morgan in the rearview mirror. "You're welcome to come, too," he said.

Morgan giggled in the backseat. "That's really kind. I'd love to, thanks." It didn't sound like Morgan at all, and Kat rolled her eyes, knew her friend wanted to come for one thing and one thing only: to figure out for herself what was going on between Kat and Sam.

Twenty minutes later, they turned left onto Montrose Street and pulled up next to a small Victorian, white with red shutters and a gleaming black door. To some, it may look like a tired old house, but to Kat, it just looked like home.

Several cars already lined the curb where Sam pulled in and got out of the car. He let Morgan out and then came around to the passenger side with Kat's crutches. They walked up to the house together, his hand on her back.

The summer wind blew gently, kicking up the scent of freshly mowed grass and a neighbor's barbecue. Just for one day, Kat wanted to set everything aside and forget all that had happened.

She glanced at Sam.

Well, maybe not *everything* that had happened.

Sam pushed open the door and gestured for Kat to enter before him. The sound of chatter and laughter circled through the house, and the clinking of dishes and running of sink water beckoned them to the kitchen.

"Come in, come in," Alice called. "We're having dinner out on the deck today. It's too pretty to stay inside."

Kat stepped into the tiny kitchen, and a woman with a shiny brunette bob and a radiant smile came into her view. She extended a hand. "Pleased to meet you. I'm Dawn."

"Mom, this is Kat," Sam added. "And her friend Morgan."

"We heard all about the cruise. We're so thankful you're all right."

Kat sensed Dawn's sincerity and immediately felt at home. "I have your son to thank. If he hadn't been there, I'm not sure if I would be standing here today."

She saw a glint of pride in Dawn's eyes—and something else, a certain sadness. It reminded Kat of the way her father had often looked at her in the years after her mother passed away. "He's always been a hero."

"Mom."

She shrugged. "Sorry, honey. It's just the truth. Anyway…" She looked back at Kat and Morgan. "Welcome. Make yourself at home. You go find somewhere comfortable to sit, Kat. Let us do everything."

Outside, the backyard was small but homey, fenced in with mature trees towering over the deck. A well-kept garden lined the back fence, and a wrought-iron bench settled between two weeping willows. Two long tables were set straight down the deck, from one end to another, plates, napkins and condiments set along the center.

"Mark, come on over here and meet our guests," Dawn called. Sam's father moved away from the grill, wiping his palms on a pink polka-dot apron, and Kat tried not to laugh.

He was a tall guy with broad shoulders, fit, and she guessed he was in his midfifties. He wore an open smile on his face and looked completely at ease in his pink apron as he crossed the short distance to the table, where everyone else had begun to take their seats.

"Welcome, glad to have you," he said, extending a hand. "You must be Kat."

She nodded, wondering just how much everyone had heard about her from Alice. "Thanks for having me." She looked toward the full table, and Dawn jumped in to help with introductions.

Finally, Kat and Morgan sat down at the table. Kat made an effort to remember all the new faces and names. Emily's dark-haired son was Parker, and they were sitting next to a line of Sam's other three sisters, fraternal twins Jules and Leah along with the oldest sister, Meg. Sam's brother, Cody, stood by the grill with his father, and Dawn and Alice took their places at the far end of the table. Mark said grace and the food was passed around in quick succession.

Morgan nudged Kat's foot under the table, quirking a big grin of approval, and as the conversation flowed, Kat relaxed and enjoyed something she'd never really experienced before. Family.

She had been well loved and she'd never considered herself lonely growing up, but there was something warm and beautiful about family coming together like this.

She glanced around at the sea of faces and wondered what their stories were. Her gaze settled on Sam, and she realized he was watching her watch them. He winked, and Kat's pulse beat a little faster.

"So, you're Morgan, right?" Em asked from across the table, and Morgan perked up at her name.

"Yes."

"We've heard just about every detail between Grandma and Sam, but there's something none of us could figure out."

"What's that?" Morgan asked.

"How did you escape?"

A dark look passed through Morgan's eyes, and Kat's throat went dry.

"Sam said part of the interview was locked, and even the security officer on the ship couldn't access it," Em pressed.

"You don't have to answer that," Dawn said smoothly from next to her youngest. "We're all a little on the nosy side, I'm afraid." She nudged her daughter, but Em just shrugged.

"No, it's okay," Morgan said. "I'd worked out an escape plan, but I hadn't gotten the courage to go for it. Then the men who had taken me showed me a photo on one of their cell phones. It was a picture of Kat. In the infirmary. It was their way of threatening me, of showing me that they had her at their mercy, unless I told them what they wanted to hear."

She set her fork down and took a sip of lemonade then, smiled good-naturedly as the family hung on her every word. "I was desperate," she said simply. "Once I saw that picture of Kat, I knew I had to escape. No matter what. I needed to get to Kat."

She looked over at Kat, her eyes holding back tears. "We're not just friends," she said. "We're sisters. If anything had happened to her, I never would have forgiven myself."

"So, you…" Em prodded.

"I waited for an opportunity, in the middle of the night," Morgan said. "Used a lamp to knock out the guy they'd left to guard me, and I was free."

"That is amazing," Em said with excitement.

The young girl obviously couldn't tell that Morgan was lying, but Kat could. She could tell by the way her friend's gaze flitted around the yard and back to her plate, not meeting anyone's eyes. And Kat wondered what Morgan had really done to escape. Realized she may never know. Secrets had grown between Kat and her friend, and she hoped they would find a way to put everything behind them and rebuild their friendship.

Soon enough, she let her worries fade away as conversation flowed again, and laughter echoed through the yard. Dinner passed quickly, the sun dipping behind the willow trees in the backyard. Sam's sisters and mother began to clear dishes from the table, Morgan pitching in, as well. Kat pushed herself up and began to stack cups, but Sam stopped her.

"They've got it." He held out a hand. "Come sit with me."

Kat left her crutches, leaning on Sam as he led her across the lawn, the night air warm and breezy, the scent of honeysuckle drifting across the yard from Alice's garden.

Sam helped Kat sit on the bench under the willows, then took a seat next to her.

"That was some family barbecue," Kat said. "Do you do this a lot?"

Sam smiled over at her. "One Sunday a month," he said. "And on special occasions."

Kat looked back at him, wondering what he meant. "Did I miss something? Is it a birthday? An anniversary?"

His hand came up, tenderly stroked the side of her jaw. "A new beginning."

Kat stilled, heart flaring with hope.

"From the moment I walked out of that hospital, I started missing you," Sam continued. "And I had to ask myself, how can I miss someone I've only known a few days?"

She'd missed him, too. But she couldn't say the words, mesmerized by the touch of his hand on her neck, the softness in his gaze.

"Then I figured it out."

Kat blinked. "What?"

"Why I missed you." He grinned. "In a matter of days, I saw you at your best, all dressed up and flawless, playing the piano like I've never heard anyone play. And I saw you devastated, when we thought the worst for Morgan. I've watched you cry and get angry."

"You've seen me without makeup, and all banged up," Kat added with a laugh, her hand coming up to the tender bruise on her cheek.

Sam smiled. "I've seen your strength and your faith, your kindness and how easily you forgive. It usually takes a long time to really know someone, but we've only had a week, and I *do* know you, Kat."

He dropped his hand from her neck and slid it over hers on the bench. "And I love you." He grinned, his dimple appearing. "Go ahead. Call me crazy."

Kat laughed, heart overflowing with happiness. "If you're crazy, then so am I," she said. "Because I love you, too."

His gaze dropped to her lips, and Kat's eyes fluttered closed as he bent toward her. His lips brushed hers and sent a river of heat coursing through her veins. She pressed in closer, slipped her arms around his waist and welcomed the deepening kiss.

An appreciative whistle sounded from the house, and Kat pulled back, cheeks hot and heart racing.

"Looks like we have an audience," Sam whispered.

Faces peered out from the open windows at the back of Alice's house, and Alice stood just outside the back door, tablecloth in hand.

"Welcome to the family, Kathryn!" she called before walking back into the house.

"I think we have my grandmother's blessing," Sam said, a teasing glint in his eyes. And he bent to kiss her again.

* * * * *

Dear Reader,

When Sam and Kat meet on board the *Jade Princess*, they're both still reeling from loss, and they can't stop looking back. Back at the loved ones left behind, back at the way life used to be, both prisoners of their own grief. But when danger greets them on the open seas, they're forced to focus on today, and the blinders of mourning must come off so they can stay alive—and fall in love.

In Isaiah, chapter forty-two, God assures us that even when we can't see around the corner, even when we don't know where to turn, *He* is ever-seeing. In our blindness, He guides us. In our darkness, He is our light. Verse sixteen reads: "I will lead the blind by ways they have not known, along unfamiliar paths I will guide them; I will turn the darkness into light before them and make the rough places smooth."

Undercurrent is a story of darkness turned to light, rocky paths made smooth and healing after loss. It's also a story of new beginnings.

Thanks for reading, and I'd love to hear from you. Visit my website at www.sarakparker.com or drop me a note at parker.sarak@gmail.com.

Sara K. Parker

Questions for Discussion

1. Samuel West shoulders a burden of misplaced guilt over the death of his wife and their unborn daughter. Have you ever experienced a sense of guilt over something that you knew, logically, you were not responsible for? How did you let it go and find peace again?

2. Kathryn Brooks reads from the book of Psalms one night, and the words bring her an immediate sense of rest and calm. Scripture tells us the Word of God is living and active. When have you experienced the living quality of God's Word in your life?

3. Sam has a very strong sense of family, whereas Kat longs for the idea of family she's never experienced. How did their backgrounds shape their views on family?

4. Isaiah 42:16 says "I will turn their darkness into light before them and make the rough places smooth." How does that Scripture relate to your life?

5. From a young age, Kat found solace through the piano. What do you do to find balance when life throws curveballs? Is there something you used to enjoy that you'd like to pick up again?

6. Sam and Kat were trapped together on a cruise ship in the middle of the Atlantic Ocean. Just for kicks, if you had to be trapped somewhere fighting for your life alongside the man of your dreams, where would it be?

COMING NEXT MONTH FROM
Love Inspired® Suspense

Available February 3, 2015

TO SAVE HER CHILD
Alaskan Search and Rescue • by Margaret Daley
When Ella Jackson's son goes missing, she'll stop at nothing
to bring him home. She turns to a brooding former soldier
to help track down the kidnapper before Ella is the next
to disappear.

FUGITIVE TRACKDOWN
Bounty Hunters • by Sandra Robbins
Bounty hunter Adam Knight doesn't hesitate when his
sister's best friend needs his help. The man who murdered
Claire Walker's father wants her dead...and Adam is her
only hope for survival.

TAKEN • by Lisa Harris
Kate Elliot trails her niece's kidnapper to Paris and teams up
with FBI agent Marcus O'Brian. Together, they must stay steps
ahead of the culprit, who is now after them as well.

PLAIN PERIL • by Alison Stone
Hannah Wittmer's Amish country homecoming is less than
welcome. Someone killed her nieces' mother...and Hannah
and her newfound protector Sheriff Spencer Maxwell are the
next targets.

SILENT HUNTER • by Maggie K. Black
Nicky Trailer is trapped on an island with a killer and the man
who broke her heart. Will Luke Wolf be able to save her life
and redeem her trust?

MANHUNT • by Lisa Phillips
When a fugitive escapes their custody, deputy US marshals
Eric Hanning and Hailey Shelder must battle floodwaters and
bullets in order to stay alive.

LISCNM0115

REQUEST YOUR FREE BOOKS!
2 FREE RIVETING INSPIRATIONAL NOVELS
PLUS 2 FREE MYSTERY GIFTS

Love Inspired®
SUSPENSE

YES! Please send me 2 FREE Love Inspired® Suspense novels and my 2 FREE mystery gifts (gifts are worth about $10). After receiving them, if I don't wish to receive any more books, I can return the shipping statement marked "cancel." If I don't cancel, I will receive 4 brand-new novels every month and be billed just $4.74 per book in the U.S. or $5.24 per book in Canada. That's a savings of at least 21% off the cover price. It's quite a bargain! Shipping and handling is just 50¢ per book in the U.S. and 75¢ per book in Canada.* I understand that accepting the 2 free books and gifts places me under no obligation to buy anything. I can always return a shipment and cancel at any time. Even if I never buy another book, the two free books and gifts are mine to keep forever.

123/323 IDN F5AC

Name	(PLEASE PRINT)	

Address		Apt. #

City	State/Prov.	Zip/Postal Code

Signature (if under 18, a parent or guardian must sign)

Mail to the Harlequin® Reader Service:
IN U.S.A.: P.O. Box 1867, Buffalo, NY 14240-1867
IN CANADA: P.O. Box 609, Fort Erie, Ontario L2A 5X3

**Are you a current subscriber to Love Inspired Suspense books
and want to receive the larger-print edition?
Call 1-800-873-8635 or visit www.ReaderService.com.**

* Terms and prices subject to change without notice. Prices do not include applicable taxes. Sales tax applicable in N.Y. Canadian residents will be charged applicable taxes. Offer not valid in Quebec. This offer is limited to one order per household. Not valid for current subscribers to Love Inspired Suspense books. All orders subject to credit approval. Credit or debit balances in a customer's account(s) may be offset by any other outstanding balance owed by or to the customer. Please allow 4 to 6 weeks for delivery. Offer available while quantities last.

Your Privacy—The Harlequin® Reader Service is committed to protecting your privacy. Our Privacy Policy is available online at www.ReaderService.com or upon request from the Harlequin Reader Service.
We make a portion of our mailing list available to reputable third parties that offer products we believe may interest you. If you prefer that we not exchange your name with third parties, or if you wish to clarify or modify your communication preferences, please visit us at www.ReaderService.com/consumerchoice or write to us at Harlequin Reader Service Preference Service, P.O. Box 9062, Buffalo, NY 14269. Include your complete name and address.

LIS13R

SPECIAL EXCERPT FROM

Love Inspired.
SUSPENSE

A woman's young son has gone missing.
Can he be found?

Read on for a preview of TO SAVE HER CHILD
by Margaret Daley, the next book in her
ALASKAN SEARCH AND RESCUE series.

"What's wrong, Ella?" Josiah's dark blue eyes filled with concern.

Words stuck in her throat. She fought the tears welling in her. "My son is missing," she finally squeaked out.

"Where? When?" he asked, suddenly all business.

"About an hour ago at Camp Yukon. I hope you can help look for him."

"Let's go. My truck is outside." Josiah fell into step next to her.

Ella slid a glance toward him, and the sight of Josiah, a former US marine, calmed her nerves. She knew how good he was with his dog at finding people. Robbie would be all right. She had to believe that. The alternative was unthinkable.

He opened the back door for his dog, Buddy, then quickly moved to the front door for Ella. "I'll find Robbie. I promise."

The confidence in his voice further eased her anxiety. Ella climbed into the cab with Josiah's hand on her elbow.

As he started the engine, Ella ran her hands up and down her arms. But the chill burrowed its way into the marrow of her bones, even though the temperature was sixty-five.

Josiah glanced at her. "David will get plenty of people to scour the whole park. Do you have anything with Robbie's scent on it?"

"I do. In my car."

He backed up to her black Jeep Wrangler. "Where?"

"Front seat. A jacket he didn't take with him."

Josiah jumped out of the truck to get it before Ella had a chance to even open her door.

He returned quickly with Robbie's brown jacket in his grasp.

He gave it to Ella. "This will help Buddy find your son."

Ella leaned forward, staring out the windshield at the sky. Dark clouds drifted over the sun. "Looks like we'll have a storm late this afternoon."

Josiah's strong jawline twitched. "We can still search in the rain, but let's hope that the weatherman is wrong."

Ella closed her eyes. She had to remain calm and in control. That was one of the things she'd always been able to do in the middle of a search and rescue, but this time it was her son.

"Ella, I promise you," Josiah said. "I won't leave the park until we find your son."

Will Robbie be found before nightfall?
Pick up TO SAVE HER CHILD to find out.
Available February 2015, wherever
Love Inspired® Suspense books and ebooks are sold.

"Are you hurt?"

Dorcas froze. She didn't recognize this stranger's voice.
Frantically, she attempted to cover her bare shins. "I'm
caught," she squeaked out. "My dress…"

"*Ne, maedle*, lie still."

She squinted at him in the sunshine. This was no lad,
but a young man. She clamped her eyes shut, hoping the
ground would swallow her up.

She felt the tension on her dress suddenly loosen.

"There you go."

Before she could protest, he was lifting her out of the
briars.

He cradled her against him. "Best I get you to Sara and
have her take a look at that knee. Might need stitches." He
started to walk across the field toward Sara's.

Dorcas looked into a broad, shaven face framed by
shaggy butter-blond hair that hung almost to his wide
shoulders. He was the most attractive man she had ever
laid eyes on. He was too beautiful to be real, this man
with merry pewter-gray eyes and suntanned skin.

*I must have hit the post with my head and knocked
myself silly*, she thought.

"I can…" She pushed against his shoulders, thinking she should walk.

"*Ne*, you could do yourself more harm." He shifted her weight. "You'll be more comfortable if you put your arms around my neck."

"I…I…" she mumbled, but she did as he said. She knew that this was improper, but she couldn't figure out what to do.

"You must be the little cousin Sara said was coming to help her today," he said. "I'm Gideon Esch, her hired man. From Wisconsin."

Little? She was five foot eleven, a giant compared to most of the local women. No one had ever called her *little* before.

"You don't say much, do you?" He looked down at her in his arms and grinned.

Dorcas nodded.

He grinned. "I like you. Do you have a name?"

"Dorcas. Dorcas Coblentz."

"You don't look like a Dorcas to me."

He stopped walking to look down at her. "I don't suppose you have a middle name?"

"Adelaide."

"Adelaide," he repeated. "Addy. You look a lot more like an Addy than you do a Dorcas."

"Addy?" The idea settled over her as easily as warm maple syrup over blueberry pancakes. "Addy," she repeated, and then she found herself smiling back at him.

Will Addy fall for the handsome Amish handyman?
Pick up A MATCH FOR ADDY to find out!
Available February 2015,
wherever Love Inspired® books and ebooks are sold.

SPECIAL EXCERPT FROM

Love Inspired HISTORICAL

Newly returned Duke Caldwell is the son of her family's enemy—and everyone knows a Caldwell can't be trusted. But when Duke is thrown from his horse, Rose Bell must put her misgivings aside to help care for the handsome rancher.

Read on for a sneak peek of
BIG SKY HOMECOMING
by Linda Ford

"You must find it hard to do this."

"Do what?" His voice settled her wandering mind.

"Coddle me."

"Am I doing that?" Her words came out soft and sweet, from a place within her she normally saved for family. "Seems to me all I'm doing is helping a neighbor in need."

"It's nice we can now be friendly neighbors."

This was not the time to point out that friendly neighbors did not open gates and let animals out.

Duke lowered his gaze, freeing her from its silent hold. He sipped the tea. "You're right. This is just what I needed. I'm feeling better already." He indicated he wanted to put the cup and saucer on the stool at his knees. "I haven't thanked you for rescuing me. Thank you." He smiled.

She noticed his eyes looked clearer. He was feeling better. The tea had been a good idea.

"You're welcome." She could barely pull away from his gaze. Why did he have this power over her? It had to be the brightness of those blue eyes…

What was she doing? She had to stop this. She resolved to not be trapped by his look.

Who was he? Truly? A manipulator who said the feud was over when it obviously wasn't? A hero who'd almost drowned rescuing someone weaker than him in every way?

He was a curious mixture of strength and vulnerability. Could he be both at the same time? What was she to believe?

Was he a feuding neighbor, the arrogant son of the rich rancher?

Or a kind, noble man?

She tried to dismiss the questions. What difference did it make to her? She had only come because he'd been injured and Ma had taught all the girls to never refuse to help a sick or injured person.

Apart from that, she was Rose Bell and he, Duke Caldwell. That was all she needed to know about him.

But her fierce admonitions did not stop the churning of her thoughts.

Pick up BIG SKY HOMECOMING
by Linda Ford,
available February 2015 wherever
Love Inspired® Historical books and ebooks are sold.